THE THEORY OF CLOUDS

THE

THEORY

OF

CLOUDS

Stéphane Audeguy

Translated from the French by Timothy Bent

Harcourt, Inc.

ORLANDO   AUSTIN   NEW YORK   SAN DIEGO   LONDON

© Editions Gallimard, Paris, 2005
English translation copyright © 2007 by Timothy D. Bent

www.HarcourtBooks.com

This is a work of fiction. Names, characters, places, organizations,
and events are the products of the author's imagination or are
used fictitiously, and any resemblance to actual persons, living
or dead, events, or locales is entirely coincidental.

This is a translation of *La théorie des nuages*

Library of Congress Cataloging-in-Publication Data
Audeguy, Stéphane.
[Théorie des nuages. English]
The theory of clouds/Stéphane Audeguy;
translated from the French by Timothy Bent.
p.   cm.
I. Bent, Timothy.   II. Title
PQ2701.U34T48413   2007
843'.92—dc22   2007004402
ISBN 978-0-15-101428-6

Text set in Requiem
Designed by April Ward

Printed in the United States of America
First U.S. edition
A C E G I K J H F D B

CONTENTS

PART I

The Study of the Skies

What a glorious morning is this for clouds!
—*John Constable*

All children become sad in the late afternoon, for they begin to comprehend the passage of time. The light starts to change. Soon they will have to head home, and to behave, and to pretend.

On a Sunday in June, sometime around 5 P.M., the Japanese couturier Akira Kumo was speaking with a young woman whom he had just hired to catalogue his book collection. Kumo and the young woman were sitting in the loftlike top floor of Kumo's *hôtel particulier* on Rue Lamarck in Paris; it was here that he had installed his library. The windows, including those in the north-facing bay windows that led to a small balcony overlooking the street, were made of double-paned glass, filtering out damaging rays and urban noises while offering a commanding view of the lead-gray Paris roofline. Above the roofline was an expanse of sky in which the clouds, always the same and always changing, drifted by, indifferent to the landscape over which they passed. Virginie Latour was examining the spines of books. She was only half listening to what the couturier was telling her—something about London at the turn of the nineteenth century. When he started talking about clouds, however, Virginie offered him her full attention.

In the early years of the nineteenth century, Kumo told Virginie, a number of unheralded and seemingly ordinary men across Europe began gazing up at clouds in a way that was serious and respectful yet also filled with longing. They looked at clouds as if they were in love with them. One was an Englishman named Luke Howard.

Luke Howard lived in London, where he worked in an apothecary. He also belonged to the Society of Friends, known more commonly as the Quakers. Howard was the kind of man impossible not to admire, for he devoted himself to his one god with the quiet constancy of the truly innocent. Once a week—sometimes more frequently—he took part in one of those meetings that are to Quakers what mass is to Catholics (though this is not a comparison that a Quaker would approve of; Quakers read the Bible incessantly and it says nothing regarding either clergy or pope). On November 25, 1802, Howard and his fellow Friends gathered in the small room situated directly over the laboratory where he worked during the day. They sat in a circle, in silence. Any participant in these meetings had the right to speak—so long as he had something to say. This was why, quite often and indeed typically, no one said anything at all. Now and again a line of thought might take hold. An actual discussion? A rarity. And when, most unexpected and unfortunate, an outright argument erupted, the meeting leader would immediately demand silence. Remaining silent was one of Howard's great talents, one he had nearly perfected. So admirably did he not speak that it opened up space in his capacious heart for the Creator of All Things—first and foremost—and secondly for the welfare of his fellow man and, lastly, for the study of clouds.

The meeting on that November day was by general consensus very satisfactory indeed. There are many qualities of silence—Quakers are excellent judges in the matter—and they agreed that the silence at this particular meeting had been among the very finest. When it was over, Howard accompanied the participants down to the front door to bid them good-bye. Last to take their leave were his closest friends, with whom he chatted amiably about various matters for a few minutes. One of them enquired as to whether he had decided upon the subject of the lecture he was to present at the next meeting of their scientific society. Howard replied that he had not settled upon one; there were several possibilities. He was not being truthful and his friends could sense this—Howard had no notion of how to lie—and chided him gently for it. But they didn't press him, and eventually they went on their way. Howard returned to his room, settled himself before a venerable-looking if worn desk, and set to work.

His friends had been right, of course. From the very moment he had learned it was his turn to give the next lecture, Howard knew precisely what his subject would be. Clouds. More than simply talk *about* clouds, however, he intended to speak *for* them, and in a manner never before attempted.

Until then, clouds were seen merely as symbols of something else: the gods' displeasure or delight; the weather's whims; premonitions of good or ill. They were not accorded an existence independent of anything else. Howard felt deeply that this was not how clouds ought to be understood. It was essential they be appreciated for themselves; that they be, in a word, loved.

Luke Howard looked at clouds in a way no one had since the days of antiquity: He contemplated them actively rather than passively. Clouds, he believed, were composed of a unique material that was in perpetual transformation; every cloud was the metamorphosis of another. Their formations thus needed to be seen in a whole new light. Moreover, these formations needed names. A Frenchman had previously tried to name clouds, but he used native terms for them. Howard opted for Latin, hoping that this would encourage scientists of every nationality to adopt his system.

Is it not amazing how self-evident everything seems following an invention of this magnitude? Rudolf Diesel's motor, or the principles behind fixed images established by Niepce and Daguerre. These are now so familiar to us that we can manipulate them. What is impossibly hard to imagine is that moment when a scientific discovery is first announced to the world. Whatever it is, or whatever it does, the discovery has to seem simultaneously self-sufficient and insufficient. In the case of clouds, language lies at the heart of the matter. And baptizing this new entity isn't like baptizing a person, who at birth receives a given name and a family name with which they can do whatever they want. Some drag their names through the mud; others carry theirs to the very heights of society's lists; a few manage to do both simultaneously. But entities—things—have an existence independent of a name and can go for centuries without it, though one might be out there somewhere, waiting for the scientist or the poet to seize upon it.

Discovering the name that facilitates comprehension of the thing named was Howard's great gift. Today, thanks to him and his typology, we see clouds with him: *cumulus* and *stratus, cirrus* and *nimbus*.

In 1796, at Number 2 Plough Yard in the Lombard Street neighborhood—not far from the Thames—Howard and his friends had founded a scientific organization—really a kind of debating club—they called the Askesian Society, a name deriving from the Greek *askesis,* meaning "application," chosen to encourage them in their efforts. The society's rules were quite simple. Once a year each member was required to give a lecture; in the event he could or would not, he would be fined an amount sufficient to cover the costs of the refreshments and the wood burned in the stove to heat the room. The neighborhood around Lombard Street was home to a small community of Quakers, bankers, and tradesmen, many of whom avidly followed the proceedings of the Askesian Society.

Around eight o'clock in the evening of December 6, 1802, Howard opened the door to the laboratory. He was wearing a plain, dark suit, a round hat, and black cravat; his shirt linen was white. Number 2 Plough Yard was an old building of three floors and had what some might call a forbidding appearance: The façade consisted of bare stone and its front bay windows were mostly obscured behind shutters. It had been rebuilt following the Great Fire more than a century before and untouched since. The owners had opened an apothecary on the ground floor, and during the day it hummed with activity. Howard normally could be found in the laboratory downstairs, working on preparations and tinctures, and it was in that laboratory that this meeting of the Askesian Society was convened.

By this hour the apothecary had been closed for some time. Howard went down the steps leading to the laboratory, which was located to the right of the staircase. His audience had already gathered and the room was crowded. There were five rows of five chairs, on which sat the women, children, and elderly men; along the sides and at the back of the room, their hats in their hands, were the men. Howard recognized a number of faces, including those of his fellow society founders, but their familiarity only augmented his shyness. Sitting on the right-hand side, as was their custom, were his closest associates—William Allen, a doctor, and William Haseldine Pepys, a naturalist; to their right was the society's secretary, Richard Phillips. All three wore dark suits and white shirt-linen; their hats poised on their knees.

Among those attending the lecture were merchants and businessmen, Jews and gentiles alike, hopeful for an opportunity to learn information that might prove useful to them. The women and children smiled at Howard, who was too anxious to return the greeting. There were a number of faces Howard did not recognize. Some, he knew, were curiosity-seekers. The previous meeting of the Askesian Society had caused a stir because it had involved a demonstration of nitrous oxide, a recently discovered gas with slightly hallucinogenic properties. The Quakers, though with serious compunction, had experimented with it, that they might compare the nature of their nervous laughter and the colors of their visions.

The laboratory, which had been swept and tidied—beakers and vials arranged in neat rows along shelves—suddenly seemed foreign to Howard. He began to speak, his voice husky and impassioned. Soon the children in the audience put their heads on their mothers' laps and began to fall asleep. Those who had been hoping for a repeat of the nitrous oxide episode noisily made their disappointed way toward the door. Those who remained stayed alert; a few took in what Howard was telling them.

Clouds could be classified into three basic groups, he told them. One group existed high above them all, stretching across the sky like cat scratches or plumes, either in long parallel lines or in wider, diaphanous swaths; these Howard called "hair wisps," or, in Latin, *cirrus*. Other clouds appeared heavier, massing themselves along the horizon, from where they played with the sun's rays; so monumental could their accumulations become that Howard designated them as "heaps," or *cumulus*. And in England clouds sometimes formed an unbroken sheet, blotting out the blue of the sky entirely. When they reached the ground they were known as fog; this group was like a "layer," or *stratus*. Completing the series were the *nimbus*, Latin for "rain," which Howard designated as a mixed type that could also be called *cumulo-cirro-stratus*.

The lecture, a huge success, was published a year afterward as a pamphlet bearing the title, "Essay on the Modification of Clouds," and illustrated with some basic but illuminating pencil drawings. One sure indication of its influence was that the British scientific community henceforth adopted Howard's cloud vocabulary. In the years that followed, and to this very day, Howard's nomenclature, though occasionally emended, has never been supplanted and remains in use throughout the world. We've simply forgotten who invented it.

How true that is for so many inventions, Kumo told Virginie, even the really famous ones. The invention eclipses the inventor, unless, that is, he takes charge of his own publicity, goaded into it by jealous colleagues or an ambitious spouse. By the time Howard finally became celebrated in meteorological circles (which, like all such communities, contained circles within circles) he had gone on to, or rather returned to, other occupations, occupations he believed would bring him infinitely greater rewards than cloud naming. These consisted of service to his God, Who required of him charitable deeds; the dissemination of the Bible into all lands and in all the known languages; and ceaseless vigilance to the welfare of his immortal soul. Howard would never publish anything again in the field of meteorology, excepting a single tome, a synthesis of thirty years spent observing the skies above his favorite city, and entitled *The Climate of London.*

Once a week for the rest of his life, most often on Sundays, Howard went for a long walk, setting off early from the Lombard Street neighborhood. Over his shoulder was a satchel; he used a walking stick, due to an old injury that continued from time to time to pain him. Within the space of an hour, proceeding at a brisk pace, he reached the village of Hampstead, which he circled on the left-hand side. His destination was the Heath, with its green hills and high pastures. Howard always entered the Heath through the southeast gate. From there, weather and season dictated his choice of itinerary. In rain he would take the wooded path along the Highgate ponds; under the protection afforded by the oak trees he would stand motionless, watching the clouds race toward the south. In clear weather, summer or winter, he climbed Parliament Hill, from which one can trace the curve of the Thames, and indeed that of the City of London itself. But Howard hadn't come to admire the commanding view of the horizon. Once he had made certain he was unobserved, he took a waxed piece of canvas from his satchel and settled down onto it amidst the tall grasses that covered the summit on either side of the pathway. Opening his eyes as wide as he could, he watched each cloud glide across the English sky, noting with pleasure its place in his classification. The thought that one day someone would alter his classification, or even that it might be abandoned altogether, was enough to make him tremble with anxiety. Eventually, abashed by his own vanity, he climbed back down Parliament Hill and returned to his friends and family, back to London and its busy goings-on, giving thanks to God for having made clouds, and for having conferred upon one of His servants the great honor of assigning their names.

Kumo stopped speaking and rose to his feet. Virginie got up as well. He accompanied her in the elevator leading to the ground floor of his house and said good-bye.

It was only while being fussed over by Kumo's staff that Virginie understood that she'd been hired. She couldn't say why. All Monsieur Kumo had talked about was clouds, she told the staff. One replied that maybe she should let him decide the manner in which he wished to proceed with organizing his library. Virginie didn't respond. She was handed an envelope, which she put in her pocket. It was eight o'clock in the evening but there was still daylight on Rue Lamarck. She strolled around the neighborhood, which was not one she knew, and then she headed home.

Virginie Latour had never given much thought to clouds until starting work for Akira Kumo. That is to say, like everyone else she never focused her attention upon them, except maybe once, during her last year of school; on a certain Friday morning she could still recall when she'd been writing a philosophy paper. As a student, Virginie had enjoyed abstract thought; she liked engaging in this patient and precise exercise, crowded and solitary both. After her student days were over everything happened so quickly— mass transit, shopping, housekeeping; a job. The time for thought ended because thinking is hard work and can be done only under the right conditions. You need quiet, free time, a regular schedule, and discipline. You have to train yourself. At least in theory you can think anywhere and while doing anything, such as when you're pushing a shopping cart around a department store. But the background music distracts you, the lights glare, and small but discernible changes in temperature between the women's wear department and home appliances can give you a headache. But Virginie had sworn she wouldn't give up trying. She was afraid that once she started a career she would never get to think at all. Every week, snuggling on her couch, she devoted a half hour to thinking. The same thing happened every time: She dozed off.

Like the vast majority of people, Virginie never found her calling in life. The closest thing she had to a passion was for the English language. She became a librarian and cataloguer by default.

When she emerged from Kumo's *hôtel particulier* on Rue Lamarck, following that first interview—if that's what it was—with her new employer, Virginie lifted her eyes and looked at the clouds. A familiar sensation came over her, one that both exhilarated and frustrated her. Whenever she learned something new about someone—such as from a documentary about a famous writer on TV or a magazine article about a painter—everything about that writer or painter suddenly seemed fascinating. She headed straight off to the Louvre or the Quai d'Orsay or some historic landmark, prepared to gaze with fresh eyes. Yet, when alone and face-to-face with whatever it was that had inspired her to make the trip, she turned torpid and listless, knowing and feeling nothing.

Observing the clouds about which Akira Kumo had spoken for nearly two full hours, Virginie tried to remember Luke Howard's terms for them and couldn't. She was being lazy, she told herself. If she tried hard enough the names would come to her. In her pocket she felt the envelope that had been handed to her and slid it to the bottom of her purse. She knew it contained money. She had wanted to give it back.

She would return it when she went back the following Monday, which was the day Kumo asked her to come again, at two o'clock in the afternoon. That meant that for an entire week she wouldn't have to go back to the library where she normally worked. It was a welcome change in routine.

In 1821, Kumo recounted to Virginie at their meeting that following Monday, the most celebrated man of letters in all of Europe wished to make himself known to the man who had named the clouds. This most illustrious figure served as an advisor to the Grand Duke of Weimar, and every morning in his journal he noted with precision the speed and direction of the wind, the configuration of the clouds, and the air temperature in the duchy. He had been using Howard's classification for quite some time. Johann Wolfgang von Goethe was seventy-three years old, an elderly man, yet his creative spirits were undimmed and he remained Europe's greatest poet and one of its most eminent scientists.

Over the course of years, in what was an open secret, and with an intoxicating sense that he would astonish the entire world with it, Goethe had been developing a science he called Morphology, which posited that all of Nature's forms followed certain recurring principles, principles that reflected the will of the Creator. This new science would thus celebrate the divine order of things. The water contained within his body would disperse when he was buried, some leaching into the soil and some evaporating into the air. Imagining that his mortal remains would nourish plants and feed tiny insects consoled Goethe when he thought of death. He even imagined that the brain of man was like a cloud, and thus that clouds represented the heavenly seats of thought, connecting the human and the divine. Perhaps thought hadn't developed, as some argued, in a block-by-block manner, like some slowly rising stone edifice; perhaps its development more closely resembled those cloudy arborescences he dearly loved to watch in the endlessly changing skies over Weimar. Goethe could sometimes shock even himself, and was careful to restrict thoughts such as these to pen and paper and not consign them to the printing press. Thoughts were like harlots: One might frequent such creatures from necessity but should do so furtively and wordlessly.

One evening, on the second to the last day of the year 1821, Goethe wrote in his notebook that a conflict between the upper and lower regions of the atmosphere early that morning had precipitated a snow flurry; until midday, the wind, coming from the northwest, had ushered in *stratus* clouds, which, in the early afternoon, had brought hail storms; the evening had turned beautiful but chilly, the clouds having been reabsorbed, apart from a few *cirrus*.

He wrote a letter to one of his London correspondents, a certain Christian Hüttner, a diplomat from Weimar serving in the British capital, asking him to find out whatever he could about Luke Howard. This wouldn't prove difficult, Goethe assured Hüttner, given Professor Howard's prominence among the science academies of his native country. A request from Goethe was not something to linger over; the obliging Hüttner immediately sought out his scholar friends, then visited a number of seats of scientific learning. To his despair the poor man could find out nothing; no one seemed to have heard of Luke Howard. Hüttner was about to give up when he chanced to meet a Quaker who said that he knew someone of that name—an extremely pious man who, to his knowledge at least, would never spend his time on something as trivial as clouds. Thus, seventeen years after he had authorized the publication of "Essay on the Modification of Clouds," Howard received a letter—polished and a little flowery—from the Honorable Christian Hüttner, consul, begging to inform him that Johann Wolfgang von Goethe himself wished to make his, Luke Howard's, acquaintance, having for so long admired his work, and that Goethe hoped to publish something that might express the degree of this admiration. Howard read and reread the letter, then put it back in the envelope, examining the postal markings closely. He took what seemed to him the most reasonable course of action with hoaxes of the sort and, with a smile, tore it up. He gave the matter no further thought.

Six months later, when he had received the poems Goethe had composed in his honor, and when his friends had attested to the fact that a German translation of "Essay on the Modification of Clouds" had indeed been under-taken, the poor apothecary, aghast at what he had done, quickly acceded to the great Goethe's request for informa-tion about the inventor of the classification that he had just had published in his magazine. Howard penned a brief autobiographical note. As one might expect, he spoke a little bit about himself, somewhat more about clouds, and a great deal about God.

Did Luke Howard and Goethe meet? Virginie had been expressly warned by Kumo's staff not to ask her employer questions, but the question just came out. Kumo seemed unperturbed by it. He replied that it was indeed very possible that Howard and Goethe had met. He had himself established this very possibility through his research in a number of documents housed right here in his personal collection, particularly Goethe's private letters and a diary Howard kept during his one and only trip to the continent.

In 1816, accompanied by two Quaker colleagues, Howard journeyed up the Rhine. He arrived at the gates of the Swiss city of Schaffhausen, in the region of the same name, sometime around eleven o'clock in the evening. The gates had been closed for many hours. He and his companions had had no choice but to call the guard and engage in a long discussion with him before eventually being allowed to enter. Under the guard's escort, they reached the inn where they were to lodge for the night. At first light the next morning, this small group of pious travelers read from the Holy Scriptures. Then they sat together for a long period of silence, watched with discrete admiration by the inn's staff, which had never before waited upon such unusual visitors.

Howard had not brought his companions to Schaffhausen by mere chance. It was here that the Rhine, swollen by the glacial waters of Lake Constance, cascaded several hundred feet over a rocky precipice. These falls were said to be sublime. From the village's southern gates Howard, unaccompanied, followed the path to the cataract. A bridge crossed the river some three hundred feet further up. Howard reached the place in an hour and leaned over the dark stone parapet. Below him the river seemed to disappear into iridescent mists, the water cascading at the place where the land seemed suddenly and brutally to come to an end. There were three small islands in the river, like stranded shipwreck survivors, overgrown with lush vegetation of a green so intense it was nearly blue. The roar was thunderous, yet Howard couldn't prevent himself from wishing to be nearer to it. He crossed the bridge to the river's eastern bank, where there was a view of the entire valley. His face was slapped by spray. Intoxicated by the water's continuous roar, he headed along a footpath that wound down the cliff and beneath the falls and led to an outcropping on which someone had built a rail fence. Now he was but a few feet away from the water thundering past him; it seemed black and almost solid. Howard was struck deeply not only by the heart-wrenching beauty of the physical world but by its indifferent power. Here was Nature's joyful exuberance. As he always did at such moments he offered thanks to his Savior and, alone with the falls and his ecstasy, launched into a fervent hymn of praise.

Just then, off to Howard's left, a group of young gentlemen and ladies began to approach. They were far from silent, and Howard had to force back uncharitable thoughts concerning these urban dwellers obviously enjoying their little country excursion. He observed them, unable to comprehend their babble. The young ladies were elaborately dressed,

and the gentlemen decked out in finery, parading like peacocks, leaning over the abyss and pretending to lose their
balance, causing the ladies to shriek in delighted fear. A fair
number of servants accompanied them, holding up enormous oilskin umbrellas to shield the group from the water-
fall's spray. Soon enough, the gay party grew bored and went
back up the path. Only then did Howard spy an old man,
leaning against the fence twenty or so feet away and peering
down into the watery chasm. In the days before photography
every traveler knew how to draw a little; in his journal, which
he sheltered behind a swath of his rainproof cloak, Howard
sketched the figure. After a moment the man seemed to
sense he was being observed; he broke from his reverie and,
smiling, gave Howard a small wave. Someone was calling
him. Howard realized that the stranger was part of the bois-
terous troop, as he set off in their direction with measured,
tranquil steps.

Luke Howard never realized that he had just seen Goethe;
nor, for that matter, did Goethe realize he had waved to
Howard. That is of no real importance. These solitary men
would have had nothing to say to one another; it was enough
that they had felt some silent connection in their contempla-
tion of the mists of Schaffhausen.

Kumo told Virginie that this would be enough for today
and rose to his feet.

Virginie took the elevator to the bottom floor. An assistant handed her another blue envelope as she walked out. This
time, after taking a few steps across the cobblestone courtyard toward the gate, Virginie stopped and turned around.
The assistant who had just paid her was already occupied

with something else, but another member of Kumo's staff listened politely as she explained that she was still on salary with the municipal library system and therefore really only on temporary assignment with Monsieur Kumo. The assistant asked what difference that made. Virginie further explained that technically she was still a civil servant, with all rights and privileges pertaining thereto, including a guaranteed income. Well, then, she was told, she should simply think of the money in the envelope as...remuneration. Virginie was about to push matters further but stopped herself. She recognized the look on the assistant's face; it was one she often got from people. What it said was that she should stop and think. She thanked the assistant and left.

In the Métro she counted out the bills in the envelope, which she had again slid to the bottom of her purse. The so-called remuneration amounted to a month's salary at her regular job. Like those of us who are semi-impoverished, Virginie generally thought of money in its least satisfying form: as a paycheck. This money was of a shocking new type; it was practically stolen, since she hadn't even begun to do whatever it was she was expected to do to earn it. The next morning at 9 A.M. she would go to the bank and deposit it into a savings account.

Once back in her apartment, Virginie called her boss, the associate director of the library system, using the private cell phone number he had given her, so that she could let him know how things were going with Akira Kumo. The associate director answered but for a full thirty seconds hemmed and hawed unresponsively. He had no idea who she was. As soon as she uttered the name of the couturier, however, the penny dropped. Ah! He was delighted. He talked animatedly about what a great opportunity this offered her. Virginie listened without replying, except to say yes or no. She couldn't remember whether she should call the associate director by his title or by his name. At the end of the conversation she managed to slip in the question that most haunted her. Did Monsieur le directeur (she'd opted for the formal approach) know what her new status would be? On assignment, he replied. She was on assignment.

Like the week before, Virginie had nothing to do but wait until her next meeting with Kumo. She hung up the phone, took a shower, and lay down on her foldaway bed, which had remained open since the morning. She wished she smoked; it would have helped pass the time. It was dawning on her what her new employment meant, or at least what it suggested—that she would be working for about four hours a week, and that most of this time would be taken up listening to Kumo talk about clouds or randomly examining the spines of books. The couturier didn't want to see her again until Friday. She would probably stop by her library branch sometime during the week, to check in and maybe pick up some things she would need to repair a damaged book.

Virginie couldn't yet take in the full measure of this change in her life. But she was determined, this time, to be content with it, to put off until later any further thought about what it all implied. She spent an hour daydreaming on the sofa bed, not sure what to do with herself. It was Monday but it felt like a Friday before a long weekend. Friday evenings were when Virginie performed a ritual, one she never told anyone about but whose roots reached back to her childhood. Getting up off her bed she went into the kitchen and returned with a plastic shopping bag, which she cut open with a pair of scissors before spreading it out on the sofa bed. She took off her panties and bra and positioned her midsection over the plastic. The first contact with the plastic was always unpleasant, but she'd never found anything that worked better. Then from the drawer in the side table that served as a nightstand she took out a small, hemmed silk pouch, a little larger than her hand. What she did next she did unthinkingly, so many hundreds of times had she done it before. The fact that it always worked made her feel like a slave to a sexual ritual. It troubled her that physical gratification should be tied into something so weirdly baroque and beyond her control. With her right hand she parted her pubic hair and with her left she positioned the pouch and began to rub. She instantly started to tremble. Her fingers tingled; a sweet warmth irradiated her throat and migrated down her thighs. Sometimes orgasm came quickly, and that was disconcerting; she would get up feeling flushed and ashamed. It was better, more delicious and more draining, when it happened slowly.

Afterward she would collapse, out of breath and lying still, her limbs like syrup, afloat in some place outside time, until brought back to consciousness by the sound of a phone ringing or a dog barking—and by the moist chill spreading around her loins. There was a great deal of liquid, a puddle of it, and she hated that it made her thighs and buttocks stick to the plastic. It wasn't urine; she'd tasted it. There was too much of it to be the normal secretion brought about by sexual arousal—to the degree that Virginie could judge what "normal" even meant. She didn't yet understand that those "norms" that supposedly govern the common good (*especially* those that govern the common good) are designed precisely to exclude the greatest number of people. She believed she was the only one to whom this happened. It was a relief that intercourse had never unleashed the same reaction. Gently lifting her back, Virginie unpeeled the plastic from her skin and got up off the bed. Pulling down on the center of the bag from the outside, she folded the corners and carried it into the kitchen. There she dumped the contents into the sink, rinsed the bag, and threw it away. She opened a hamper and threw in the wet silk pouch. Glancing at the time on the DVD player, she started moving more quickly; she only had a few minutes left to herself. Without getting dressed—to let the air dry her off—she folded up the sofa bed, dressed, sat down, and started to read a magazine.

First came the noise of the elevator, then the sound of keys, then the sound of the deadbolt releasing. The door opened. The young man was home. He grunted hello to Virginie, then headed off to take a shower. He was always in a foul mood before his shower. Eventually the young man returned, drying his hair with a bath towel and asking her if everything was all right. She always replied it was. And what about him? No, not really, he said, because it was Monday and Mondays sucked. Did he want some tea, she asked. A beer, he replied, and then went and got one himself, opened it, and came back with it. She was the one who wanted tea, and went into the kitchen.

The young man disappeared again and came back wearing white boxers with vertical stripes of various widths and colors: three shades of blue and two of gray. On the large blue stripe was a grinning Mickey Mouse, with his four-fingered hands, black circular ears, and stumpy feet. The young man collapsed on the couch and put his feet up on the small coffee table that had been so pretty when it was new. He turned on the local news, to find out what the weather was going to be like tomorrow. From the kitchen, Virginie told him that she was thinking of quitting her job to start something new. Then she stopped and bit her lip. She knew the young man hated it when she talked while he was watching the local news, and especially when they were about to give the weather forecast. Maybe he hadn't heard her, or maybe the forecast was for nice weather. Otherwise he was completely capable of not talking to her at all for a full hour, sometimes longer.

To Virginie's surprise, the second she stopped speaking the young man turned off the television. She heard him get up and come into the kitchen, where she was pouring hot water into the teapot, and from behind her she heard him say that he was really glad that she'd said that. Because, like, he needed a change, too, and remember how they had told each other from the beginning that they would be totally honest about it when they thought things weren't going great between them. And they're not, said the young man. She turned to face him. He wasn't looking at her but kept talking. He was telling her that he had asked his buddy Fred, the one who was going off to spend three months in Germany, for the keys to his apartment. He was going to live in Fred's place until Fred came back. They could still get together now and then.

Under normal circumstances, Virginie might have said or done something. She might have told the young man that he had gotten everything wrong, and that she had never said that they should split up when things weren't going all that great. Or she might have slapped him, because this asshole had spent an entire year talking about finding the right job and what he would do with his life when he did, and now he was leaving just when he had finally found what seemed like the right job. Instead, Virginie went into the living room. She said that she was happy that he was taking their breakup in stride. The young man finished swigging his beer in the living room and was starting to feel like things were going pretty well actually. He said that it was really for the best.

Wasn't it great that they'd managed to avoid one of those sordid scenes? Virginie continued to agree with him, and because of this he suddenly became less sure of himself. They started to have a fight. She really must be pretty fucking heartless to be taking everything so lightly. By this point, however, it was getting close to nine o'clock in the evening, and there was a Steve McQueen film on at nine he wanted to catch. He and Virginie unfolded the sofa bed and lay down. The young man watched the film. Later on, as he took off his boxer shorts, which he always did before going to sleep, he became aroused by the idea that they were breaking up. With his arm he drew Virginie close to him. She had been facing in the opposite direction but knew what he wanted. She had always loved the taste of sperm, and saw no reason to deprive herself of it now. For fun she decided to bring him to orgasm as fast as she could. He was asleep two minutes later.

By the time Virginie came home from the movies on Tuesday night, the young man had moved out. A month later, while reorganizing a drawer, she realized that she didn't have a single photograph of him. She tried to recall his face or his voice and couldn't, which seemed a little sad. In the days that followed she went for walks. She rediscovered the pleasure of riding the Métro, because now she could ride it at off-hours. She was curious about what would happen on Friday and Googled Akira Kumo.

According to the Web sites Virginie perused, Kumo was a middling celebrity: There were a thousand or so Web pages devoted to him and most of them picked up and restated—sometimes in garbled fashion—what could be found on his official site. And then there were the usual screwball sites posted by the inevitable fanatics. His name came up in some of the oddest places, and Virginie soon learned why: Over the years he had put together a wide variety of collections—collections of everything from Savoyard roasting spits to traditional saris made of raw silk to Australian opals to Gobelin tapestries to Ming vases. His most spectacular collection involved the reconstitution, in his *hôtel particulier* on Rue Lamarck, of the interior of an eighteenth-century French house: everything from teaspoons to furniture to lithographs of frolicking lovers.

Starting in 1995 the couturier began selling off his collections one by one, and each time this sent a shock wave through the microcosms of other specialists and collectors. The last items to be auctioned off at Sotheby's in London were the

Regency furniture and the lithographs by Boucher and Wat-
teau. Because the dispersal of his collections—in the space of
merely two years—had coincided with the couturier's semi-
retirement, it had fed the usual kinds of rumors: that he
was bankrupt, or had gone mad, or was dying, or all the
above. In the confusion, the commentary largely ignored one
truly remarkable thing: In September 1997, Kumo started a
new collection. That it had provoked a sudden spike in the
cost of these items hadn't concerned him. He began buying
every work on meteorology available. Before long he possessed the finest collection in private hands.

About his personal life there were relatively few known
facts. Akira Kumo had been born in Hiroshima in 1946.
When he had settled in Paris and was asked where he was
from, Kumo said "Tokyo," in order to avoid that expression
of embarrassment and pain Westerners feel when they hear
"Hiroshima." He had nothing against lying, so long as the lie
contained a higher truth. Eventually he didn't feel as if he
were lying at all. He said he had been born in Tokyo—not in
1946 but in 1960, the year he had started to learn graphic art.

Things had happened fast for Kumo. He left Japan in
1966 to begin a basic course in fashion design. He had abandoned graphic design for fashion because he had been looking for a way to leave Japan for Europe. He had not chosen
to live in France because it was a fashion center, though of
course it was, but in order to pursue a very different sort of
activity. In Tokyo whatever money he had earned from his
work—drawing bowls and silverware and furniture—he spent
on a Caucasian prostitute, a large, friendly woman with rippling
mounds of fat; she was from a Parisian suburb and began her

career in a bordello before setting up on her own. Akira had
been observing her for some time while she worked the edges
of Tokyo's red-light district. The Japanese prostitutes feigned
indifference to this outsider but in reality despised her. Akira
chose her not because he was repelled by the local profession-
als; he had always admired Japanese prostitution, which by
tradition attaches no unhealthy moral onus to sexuality. It
was simply because he preferred foreign women, and once he
started sleeping with them his tastes were confirmed. Japanese women weren't noisy or hairy enough for him. Moreover
they often played the naughty schoolgirl, which pleased their
typical clientele but held little appeal for him.

Akira was one of the few Japanese to live through the
American occupation in perfect contentment, particularly
once he had realized that, like all great militaries, the American army had been followed the entire length of the Pacific
Ocean by a long train of women attracted by the rule of the
dollar. Akira became a generous client of these women—
some were black, which he found endlessly fascinating; there
were Manchurians, and Europeans from the Dutch colonies,
particularly French and British. He liked having sex with pe-
tite women because he could hold them better; he liked having sex with large women because he could lose himself in
them; he loved those who chatted and those who were silent.
Later, once he had become rich and was in a position to pay
handsomely for whatever and whomever he wished, he would
spend many hours of bliss, his head buried between legs
spread wide to him, his aching neck bobbing up and down.

At first Akira had earned little money. In Tokyo he gained
a reputation for never refusing an assignment, and for doing

a job fast and well and cheaply. He smiled and bowed deeply when an employer commented favorably upon his work while handing him a pay envelope at the end of the week. That very night, the money would be spent in the red-light district. Early on Sunday morning, an exhausted Akira would slip silently back to the room he occupied in a boarding house for young workers and collapse on the futon mattress. He slept through the entire day, occasionally getting up to drink hot tea to suppress his hunger pangs, for he was left without a penny. Monday morning, very early, he came down to the common room, along with all the other young men, to wait for job requests to arrive. He never had to wait longer than an hour. After two years of this routine, Akira had mastered his profession.

When he landed in Paris in September 1966, Akira consulted a map of the city, scanning it for train stations, quickly noting that two were located side by side on the Right Bank. He took a room in a small hotel on the Rue Montorgueil and then headed off in the direction of these stations (the Gare du Nord and the Gare de l'Est). His efforts were rewarded immediately, for in the first street he came upon prostitutes prowling for johns. He continued on until he came to what seemed to be the Arc de Triomphe, though it was quite small. Just before he reached a large boulevard he turned to the right, into a small, dark street—Rue Blondel—in whose shadows he could make out a line of women in miniskirts and open bodices. He set his sights on a brunette who had positioned herself on a corner of Blondel and the noisy, crowded boulevard, and tried out his French. In the 1960s, in Paris, a Japanese man was an object of considerable curiosity. The women talked about him; they compared experiences. Soon he knew them all—those who worked the Ponceau Alley and those who took up stations along Rue Saint-Denis and Rue Quincampoix. He knew which women worked mornings, which worked after dark.

Given his lifestyle, the stipend allotted him by the Japanese textile union to fund his training in Paris ran out in seventeen days. By the end of September he was forced to find work. He found it in the very same Saint-Denis neighborhood he now regularly prowled, for it had as many tailors as prostitutes. He paid for the latter with money earned from the former. Akira's Paris was bordered by Boulevard de Sebastopol on the east, by Porte Saint-Denis on the north, by Rue de Turbigo on the south. The tailors he worked for made cheap clothes; he didn't care.

One day in December 1966, Akira was leaving a room in the Sainte-Foy alley, heading toward Saint-Denis. Sainte-Foy was a sordid pit; a stew of unidentifiable offal flowed in the gutters frequented by cats with ragged fur. So grim was this place, so fetid and putrid smelling, that simply being there gave him the delirious sense that now he was more than a mere tourist. He knew the real Paris, the streets most Parisians wouldn't risk venturing—and for good reason. The alley was covered halfway along its progress by a canvas canopy reeking of rancid cooking oil and semolina. A sound drew Akira's attention toward a dark corner. A man in a suit had pinned a woman to the ground and, leaning over her awkwardly, was beating her methodically in places where it would hurt most but show least—never in the face or stomach. He knew what he was doing and wasted no effort. The

unresisting woman groaned resignedly under his blows, waiting for it to be over.

Akira had the advantage of surprise when he struck the
man, who ran off, howling and sniveling and issuing vague
threats. The prostitute he had rescued immediately launched
into a stream of obscenities, which, because he still spoke
French badly—he'd tried to learn it by himself in Tokyo—
Akira didn't at first realize was directed at him. Who the fuck
did he think he was? The pimp would think they were working together. She was going to get it just because this blun-
dering fuck-up had decided to step in. By this point Akira
had become fairly established in the neighborhood and was
always greeted respectfully by the pimps. That was all finished. If he showed his face here again he'd be met with iron
bars and switchblades.

Thus ended Akira's Saint-Denis phase. He didn't care for
the other districts: Pigalle was too touristy, and the pricy call
girls around the Madeleine were the sort who dreamed of
one day marrying a client.

The incident with the pimp also deprived Akira of his income. He found employment as the third assistant to the
director of a fashion house on Avenue Montaigne. He perfected his drawing techniques on his own time—designing
dresses, trousers, suits. For weeks at a time he remained celi-
bate. This being the Paris fashion world in the 1960s, he
could easily have found companionship for an evening, or for
several evenings, had he really wanted it. The truth was he
had no heart for the sentimental and tedious comedy of se-
duction one was forced to perform to get under a woman's
dress. He focused on his work.

In the summer of 1967 Akira was sent to Amsterdam on temporary assignment as the personal assistant to a well-known French fashion designer. He ducked out of receptions as soon as he could manage it and headed straight to the red-light district, one of the few in the world without pimps. Amsterdam was his city. West of the train station, around two canals, and in the maze of the neighboring alleyways, some thousand or more prostitutes plied their trade. After this Kumo went to Amsterdam every year and spent a week there. In one day he might visit as many as half a dozen women—unless he opted to hire the services of a particular favorite for an entire afternoon.

Over the years he developed affection and respect for these women, some of whom he got to know, learning how their kids were doing in school and about their love lives. Amsterdam was the one place where Kumo could have normal conversations. Sometimes, late in the evening, if he happened to be a woman's last client, he waited while she put her things away and locked up her studio, and then he took her out to a restaurant. When the week was over, he returned to Paris and went back to work. In 1970, he started working for himself.

You have to be single-minded, Kumo said to Virginie, and single-minded in a particularly willful sort of way, to take an interest in clouds. For most people, clouds are simply there, part of the décor, not worth paying attention to. They find nothing extraordinary about clouds nor expect much from them, apart from an indication that it might rain, which they anticipate either with impatience or dread. The progress of civilization has relieved us of the duty of observing the sky. We listen to the radio or watch TV or go online to find out whether we need a raincoat. Only on rare occasions are we touched by the beauty of clouds, such as when we're lying in the grass on a Sunday afternoon and gazing up. Then and only then we might focus on them as they roll by, admiring them in a mindless sort of way. This is normal. Really thinking about something is silly—as is the desire to understand clouds.

Luke Howard had apparently started to love clouds early in his life. We don't know why. Nothing, so far as anyone

knows, predisposed him to eccentricity. He never participated in any profane activities—and didn't read poetry. As
we've seen, he belonged to the Society of Friends, whose
members some sarcastic magistrate had derisively termed
"Quakers" because they sometimes trembled at the thought
of God's might. Perhaps Howard trembled before clouds;
perhaps they gave him a delicious sense of terror and awe.
And perhaps he justified his passion for them by telling himself they were the momentary incarnations of divine perfec-
tion. At any rate the eyes he lifted to look at them were bright
with religious fervor.

He was not idle during the hours he was not working
in the apothecary, which was demanding work in any case.
Quakers might be pacifists but they are not passive. In
1816—during the same voyage to the border of Weimar and
that visit to the falls at Schaffhausen—Howard was dis-
patched to the continent, which had been devastated by the
Napoleonic wars. His mission was to distribute bibles, a duty
incumbent upon all members of the Society of Friends, and
to offer financial relief to the victims of combat, whatever
their nationality. He allowed himself two small frivolities:
that excursion to the falls and a visit to Paris, about which he
had heard so much. He arrived on Saturday, August 24, 1816,
at the Hôtel de Rastadt on Rue Neuve-des-Augustins and
hired a guide for three francs. Parisian guides, as every voy-
ager of the period well knew, doubled as police informers.
Unaware of this, Howard replied openly to the man's in-
quiries. On Sunday, he visited the Jardin des Plantes, which
was again being called the King's Garden, its pre-Revolution
name. Howard's guide grew frustrated with this odd visitor

who neither drank nor caroused, who was proving impossible to denounce. Howard sent him home with a handsome tip. That same Sunday was the *Fête du Roy.* Apart from two hours in the morning devoted to attending mass, Parisians went about their business as if it were any normal day. They gathered in the city's lecture halls, cafés, and restaurants; they walked and smoked, observing the life around them in the streets. Howard looked with sadness upon these insouciant Parisians and their placid impiety. He concluded that they could never become Quakers and thanked God he had not been born Parisian. He cut short his stay and returned to London; he would never leave the city again.

Virginie soon grew used to her new work life. Entering through the gate of Kumo's *hôtel particulier* on Rue Lamarck she would cross the cobbled courtyard, where it was always a little chilly; on the right, massive doors opened to offices humming with activity and lively debates. In a small doorway at the rear of the entry court she could see a stairway leading…she didn't know where. The elevator took her directly to the top floor. The furniture in the library was spare: A reading chair was positioned next to a simple table; in front of the bay windows that had been built into the north side was a long table, used to examine the larger volumes, and a lectern made of brushed steel. A desk chair that seemed out of place with the rest of the décor but which turned out to be surprisingly comfortable was reserved for Virginie.

The library had been designed according to its owner's specifications: A sort of airlock separated it from the rest of the building, ensuring that it remained sound-insulated and hygrometric. When she arrived, Virginie went straight over to the large bay window whose glass was so clean it seemed nonexistent. It was odd, she thought, that the architect had chosen to put the windows facing north, in the opposite direction of the Montmartre cemetery and the rest of Paris. Along this stretch of Rue Lamarck the buildings, which dated to the beginning of the last century, are two or three stories high. Kumo's therefore towered over them and the view from it was unobstructed. You could see the Saint-Ouen cemetery, the dark line of suburbs (dwarfed by the country-side beyond), and, on the right, the national stadium, an enormous bowl that seemed to arise from nowhere. Occasionally a contrail traced a delicate white line across the sky, angling off toward some unknown destination.

She would never forget her first day in that library. Virginie had thought she was alone when suddenly she became aware of someone standing on her right. She'd turned and smiled. He was a small man, wizened, almost spectral, and moved with the languid elegance of an iguana. Without introducing himself he began talking to her. Organizing a library, he had said, meant knowing about the subjects to which the books were consecrated. Soon Virginie had fallen under the spell of his resonant voice, which seemed somehow to float, while he talked and talked—about London and clouds and Luke Howard.

On her third visit Kumo was again waiting for Virginie in the library. She asked whether they shouldn't start classifying the books, but he seemed to be in no particular hurry. He had thought more about that question she had asked, he said, the one about whether Goethe and Howard ever met. He wished to return to it and to finish his thought on the subject. In the way generally intended by "meet," he explained, they had not. But in their shared love for clouds, they had. They were solitary in the way that everyone is. Our works alone mark the deserted landscapes of our lives.

To trace Howard's work on clouds we need to go to the spring of 1794, when he first started working in the apothecary. Mostly he made tinctures and bandages, enveloped in the dry sweet odor of camphor, which he grew to love. One day, just after he had gotten hold of a glass container of arsenic that had been placed on the topmost shelf reachable only by means of a ladder, the ladder slid on the waxed wood and he fell. The glass jar struck the floor before Howard did and he fell on a shard, which traveled all the way to the artery in his thigh. So great was the pain that he fainted and remained unconscious for two days. He was not expected to live. The wound, inflamed by the arsenic, became infected. Nonetheless, against every expectation, the abscesses finally began to drain, creating the most horrific odor imaginable; and after being carefully cleaned and washed, the wound began to scar. During the two days Howard was unconscious he was plunged into delirium: He had died, he dreamed, and the angels of Paradise, taking pity on him for his suffering, led him directly into Heaven. Unable to work for six weeks, he was sent home to his native Yorkshire to recuperate.

Howard had not been back to his village in years. His father greeted him coldly. He had never forgiven his son for abandoning the family farm. At the advanced age of seventy the senior Howard continued to labor in the fields and stables ten hours each day. Luke was still quite frail. The weather was growing more clement with each passing day, and he was stationed in a large wicker chair in a corner of the garden at his father's house. Because Luke was too weak to focus his eyes, a neighbor offered to read the Scriptures to him. Mariabella had been a girl of five when Luke had gone off to London. She was the daughter of a certain John Eliot, a man of slender means and dubious reputation, a sometime poacher who had raised the girl on his own, for her mother died while giving birth. Eliot doted upon his daughter. Luke listened to Mariabella giving him the divine word, which seemed as beautiful as ever; the clouds that passed overhead were, as ever, changing and eternal, and they seemed to him like silent, luminous canticles. It occurred to him that it was men who floated by and the clouds that watched. He thanked Providence for giving him this time of convalescence, and thus the chance to listen to the Book of Books. When he grew weary, he closed his eyes. Mariabella leaned over him as he dozed. When he opened his eyes he saw her face, framed against a background of deep blue. Another twelve years would pass before John Eliot, worn down by their obstinate fidelity to one another, finally permitted Luke and Mariabella to wed.

Howard's strength returned slowly and it was some time before he felt well enough to write. To sharpen his faculties and to justify the time they spent in each other's company, he taught Mariabella what he knew about botany and French, chemistry and geology. Eventually he returned to London. They spent those twelve fervent yet chaste years exchanging letters, never seeing one another for more than a week each year. When the sadness of their separation grew unbearable,

Mariabella and Luke indulged in a secret ritual: cloud-watching, for the same sky encompassed them.

Akira Kumo was satisfied with his new employee. She didn't pester him with questions about fashion, or ask about Japan and what it was like to grow up there. Whenever someone asked him about his youth, Kumo's typical response was silence. He had over time devised a simple but effective routine: Looking squarely at whoever had asked the question, he would open his mouth, as if about to say something, and then close it. The truth was that Kumo never thought about Japan. There was, however, one question to which he had no answer, and it involved his obsession with clouds. His profession had taught him that sometimes it was best not to overanalyze things, that leaving them in shadow was the right course. Yet he couldn't help feeling that an answer lay in wait for him somewhere, crouched like a beast hidden in the dark jungle of memory. He shivered at the thought that one day it might leap out at him and in one swift and terrible motion devour him whole.

Like all things so simple and sublime, clouds pose dangers. Kumo was explaining this to Virginie one day while perched on a stepladder. Men are destroyed, and destroy each other, over basic things—money or hatred. On the other hand a really complicated riddle never pushed anyone to violence; either you found the answer or gave up looking. Clouds were riddles, too, but dangerously simple ones. If you zoomed in on one part of a cloud and took a photograph, then enlarged the image, you would find that a cloud's edges seemed like another cloud, and those edges yet another, and so on. Every part of a cloud, in other words, reiterates the whole. Therefore each cloud might be called infinite, because its very surface is composed of other clouds, and those clouds of still other clouds, and so forth. Some like to lean over the abyss of these brainteasers; others lose their balance and tumble into its eternal blackness.

Who fell in? Virginie asked. She had asked another question. Kumo descended the ladder and put the stack of books he had been carrying down on the long table. He replied that painters were particularly vulnerable to the danger of clouds. Not of course the artists traditionally considered "cloud painters," such as the Italian Tiepolo or the British Constable; not even the so-called Dutch Masters. All those artists perceived the danger and never painted clouds as they really were. Instead, they cheated, and because they cheated they survived. Other painters were more reckless. They thought clouds were aerial miracles. These were the ones who couldn't see that eventually clouds would close in on them and crush them. But *who* were they? asked Virginie. Kumo replied that the best example was also the least well-known—and how often that was the case. He was an English painter known as Carmichael. No one ever knew his given name. Carmichael's papers were among his most prized possessions, said Kumo, though they had cost next to nothing to acquire. Before he died the artist had destroyed nearly all of his works, and thus remained nearly anonymous.

During the summer of 1812 Carmichael painted clouds and only clouds, and while he did so he kept a journal, the only thing written in his hand to survive. Kumo had research done on Carmichael but it had yielded little of use. Carmichael was mentioned by a number of chroniclers and memoirists at the beginning of the nineteenth century as a promising young painter. He never lived up to that promise; there was no record of his being an active painter after 1804. On the other hand the researchers did turn up a drawing "professor" by the name of Carmichael, who after 1804 and up until his death placed advertisements in the largest London daily newspapers, offering to instruct children and young women in the use of charcoal and watercolor. The aforementioned 1812 journal offers no evidence that this "professor" was the same man as the painter. The only works of Carmichael's to survive can be seen in the Victoria and Albert Museum in London. Kumo told Virginie he had gone to see them and been disappointed. They are unremarkable landscapes done in the style of Gainsborough. And yet Carmichael had noted in his journal that he had completed a hundred "sky studies," as he called them, the first dated June 1811 and the last August 2, 1812. In the margins of the journal are quite a number of sketches. There is something unforgettable about them. They give the viewer a feeling of sadness, because, rough though they are, they offer evidence that no one had ever rendered clouds with greater majesty. After August 2, 1812, Carmichael seems to have fallen victim to his avowed obsession. His "cloud period," if we can call it this, lasted for a very short period of time, and he apparently spoke to no one about it.

Initially, Carmichael had been more interested in the wind than in clouds. Of course one couldn't paint the wind, though the Chinese came the closest to capturing it; all you could paint were its effects. Carmichael studiously observed the undulations of ripening fields of wheat, the arabesques that squalls drew upon the waters of a lake; he observed how the sails of a boat were filled, and the angles the rigging made against the water; he watched wind funnels and the curves they left upon the sand dunes. At the end of the spring of 1811, however, Carmichael began harkening to the silent appeal of clouds. He found the ideal place for observing them, and it was the very same place where Luke Howard, during the same exact period, went on his Sunday walks: the Heath at Hampstead. The Heath couldn't be described as country-side, and two thousand years of civilization had wiped clean any trace of pristine wildness. But with its ponds and hills, its long lines of ancient trees, and the abrupt, dramatic views—always to be found off the trodden paths—it offered of the City of London, Hampstead had become what it would remain for the next two centuries: a walker's paradise, something that the city's parks, with their charmless rigor, would never be.

Kumo sank down in his easy chair. Virginie sat on the stepladder. Further work would wait.

Carmichael took up residence in Hampstead, in a house that he first rented and subsequently purchased. It was situated a few steps from the Heath's highest point, Parliament Hill, rising slightly under two hundred and fifty feet in altitude. He was determined to devote himself to painting clouds. His early attempts were, he felt, lamentable. He first needed to find the right medium, sheets of paper thick enough to absorb the generous layers of wash he piled on top of one another in the hope of conveying an impression of clouds' massiness. He cut these sheets up into a variety of shapes and sizes, having quickly realized that no single format could capture every kind of nebulousness. He thus discovered for himself what scientists were only beginning to grasp: that there are clouds with vertical orientation, and clouds that seem to stretch infinitely along the horizon. Though no meteorologist, Carmichael was something of an expert on clouds. The reasons were connected with his youth, though by the time of his cloud period he had broken off all ties with his family and preferred not to recall his early days.

Day after day Carmichael prowled the Heath, easel resting on his shoulder. Often he set himself up at the base of
a hill. There might be a few bathers around if he happened
to be near one of the ponds; normally, however, his only
company consisted of farm animals, a horse hitched to a
two-wheeled cart, particularly when he was in the Heath's
northern end, where it most closely resembled farmland.
Above him was the expanse of sky that sometimes seemed to
devour his canvas whole. Leaving his small, white, two-story
house before sunrise, he took with him his paint box and the
pot lid that served as his palette. He had reduced his choice
of paint to the essentials: Prussian blue powder, white, and
black charcoal. At first, he didn't paint at all; he simply stared
at the wild and unsettled expanse he wanted to capture. The
sky reveals itself to you when you approach it straight on. If
you try to take it quickly the result can be blinding—look at
one of the painter Turner's storms. On the other hand, if
you proceed too slowly, the result is cold and unfaithful, like
something produced by one of the art academies. The best
thing is to plant yourself squarely in the spot you have chosen, standing straight in front of your object, and wait.

So Carmichael waited, sometimes for hours. He wasn't
waiting for inspiration, of course, or for the clouds to assume
a more beautiful form—all cloud formations are equally fascinating when you know how to look at them. He was waiting for the painting to emerge from within him like a rising
wind, a surge in barometric pressure, taking form impercep-
tibly, exactly as clouds do. He was waiting for this power to
take control of his body, such that it might infuse the paper.

He was turning himself into a cloud, in other words. Only when the moment arrived did he paint.

Painting clouds is not easy. You have to work fast, before the sunlight and the breezes on the Heath's heights dry everything out. Carmichael brought two easels. On the first he pinned one of his sheets and applied the base, a task some painters consider beneath them, letting their apprentices do it for them. He had no apprentice, and he enjoyed this basic task. With his largest brush he applied a thin layer of white lead mixed with Prussian blue—the basis of the sky. Then he waited for the background to dry, taking in the landscape and the ever-changing sky without forcing his focus upon it. He chose his spot carefully; it was always located within the axis of the dominant winds. Then he let the clouds come to him. While the first sheet was drying, he started a second, following the same principles but working from a slightly different perspective. Once the backgrounds were finished, he painted the clouds. Patiently and rapidly he applied layer after layer of semiopaque grays, blues, and pinks. Gradually, from beneath his hand, they took form. Now had come the critical moment, the moment that both exhilarated and haunted Carmichael: deciding when the work was finished. Not knowing is the reason most painters fail. They wait too long, or they stop too soon and all you see is the painting, patterns and textures. Or they succumb to the temptation of adding just a little more over here, scratching out something over there, retouching. When they take a step back to have a look, they see instantly that rather than rendering mass they have garbled everything into one unredeemable mess.

Because Carmichael understood the challenge, he worked ceaselessly. He therefore found himself in an odd position. The problems Carmichael confronted—finishing, working in series, capturing atmosphere—were the same ones faced by the Impressionists and those who followed them. Poor Carmichael's tragedy lay in the fact that his isolation forced him to take on challenges far ahead of his time. He invariably felt that his first two attempts were failures and ripped them up, and went on to start two more, and two more after that, working until five o'clock in the evening, at which point he stopped. He retouched his works one by one, highlighting different elements with white. Back in his studio, once everything was dry, he carefully added minute amounts of the precious lapis lazuli–based blue pigments to deepen the color of the sky.

After several weeks of work Carmichael realized that contemplating clouds wasn't enough. You had to understand them as well. Seeking instruction in their science he came across the work of man named Forster, an honest but uninspired cloud popularizer. Carmichael learned that Forster had relied almost entirely on the work of a certain Luke Howard, whose classification came as an illumination to Carmichael. Howard gave him what he most wanted: names for these forms floating in the skies above Hampstead. He learned these names by heart. From then on Carmichael no longer painted clouds, he painted *cirrus* and *nimbus* and, though less often (they were less of a challenge, he felt), *stratus*. These words appeared in the titles of the works.

Important to him as the names were, Carmichael also continued to regard each and every cloud, and each configuration of the sky, as utterly unique. His cloud euphoria continued until the middle of the summer of 1811, when the notebooks assume a tone we might term religious, had Carmichael not been such a confirmed atheist. In his way, however, he was giving thanks in the only way he could to the sky—a sky emptied of all deity—that had inspired him and offered such joy. Carmichael understood that paying homage to clouds meant not painting them with precision but demonstrating his devotion. In his Hampstead solitude he approached clouds with humble piety.

One doesn't paint to make a painting, or even to be a "painter." Those who do are mere amateurs. True painters paint for more profound reasons, reasons that have nothing to do with a career. The essential thing is the relationship between his art and everything that is not the painting—in other words, the colors and flavors of the world. Starting at the age of fifteen, Carmichael passed many days on the observation platform of the largest of his father's grist mills, located at the edge of a tiny village in Yorkshire called East Bergholt. He spent hours standing up straight, looking at the sky and the horizon. Though he had always had a talent for drawing, he hadn't yet worked with paint. From some distance from East Bergholt, a traveler, during clear, calm weather, might see the five mills belonging to Carmichael's father, moving their arms in the unsettled skies of Yorkshire. The largest was the one in the center, flanked on each side by smaller mills. Carmichael was a superb observer, and that was why his father posted him on its platform. In the villages of the region he was known as the Handsome Miller. Pursued by attractive and forward women, he was too proud to give in to their advances. Keeping up appearances was good for business, so his father forced him to attend church. Young Carmichael was furious when he heard the pastor tell the congregation that the first man and woman had been chased out of their earthly paradise for their sins. How could anyone listen to such drivel? Dressed in their Sunday finest, the women stared at him dumbly. The men hated him, though Carmichael couldn't understand why; he had no interest in their wives or girlfriends. His father was rich and powerful because that's what came of owning mills at the time.

Toward the end of September each year, Carmichael senior enlisted his sons to watch the weather. As the eldest, Carmichael the younger was expected to take over the family business, except that he loved observing the weather to the same degree that he hated account books and having to pander to dealers. He loved to draw. He told himself that he would obey his father's wishes and take over running of the mills, making his art in the off-season. Everything was settled, he thought. As he stood on the mill platform, he tried to clear his mind, to better decipher the faint signs along the horizon.

In this part of the world, prosperity depended upon accurate observation. Yorkshire lived from its wheat, which it sold to London as flour, and Carmichael's father's mills were what turned the wheat into flour. The rules of grain commerce were gloriously and brutally straightforward: The first to get his flour to London's market got the best price for it. The wind was a miller's best friend and worst enemy. A steady moderate breeze was most desirable but rare in Yorkshire, and therefore millers watched the sky with utmost care. A sudden gust could destroy the windmill's sails or even break its main arm. That would be catastrophic for everyone concerned—for those who made the sacks in which the flour was shipped, and those who transported it to London's markets; for those who sold the flour in bulk as well as for those who dealt in small quantities. A miller spent his days praying for the wind either to rise or fall. At the first sign of a breeze strong enough to turn the wheels, he put everything into operation; when the breeze threatened to die down, which could disrupt the grinding and damage the process, he ordered a full stop. Without wind the mill's arms wouldn't turn; too much and they'd snap in two. The miller's job was to anticipate weather. The minute it threatened to overpower the process, he positioned the sails straight into the wind. In the event of an outright storm, he took them down.

Carmichael excelled in wind watching; his stepbrothers (his own mother had died in childbirth), Golding and James, were far less accomplished and tried to shirk their duty. Whenever their father sent them to the mill, they pretended to obey but instead went off to pick blackberries or fish for eel and gudgeon. Carmichael remained at his post. He marveled at how the sky's energy was transferred to the mill's massive stones, and he loved being guardian of this awesome power. When he saw clouds approaching he often thought of painting them, but didn't yet dare. Still, he had his favorites, and they were the ones sailors and millers call "messengers"— the smaller clouds that slide under the bigger ones and are heralds of storms and heavy weather. As soon as he realized he was deemed handsome, Carmichael was put off from painting the human face. He was tired of hearing about his own, and of people asking him to do portraits, and so he turned to the sky, even though the stupefying beauty of the clouds in motion surpassed his skills and brought him back to earth. With his friend John Dunthorne, a plumber by trade, he left for the fields and woods. Side by side, without speaking, they sketched.

There was only one man in East Bergholt capable of initiating Carmichael into the art of painting and that was Sir George Beaumont. Sir George spent most of the year in London but in warm weather took up residence in his ancestral home in Yorkshire. At the end of the summer of 1804 he happened to see a drawing hanging in a chemist's shop in East Bergholt; it was of a forest clearing half obscured by fog, rendered in graphite. It was not a polished piece of work, and revealed a number of technical errors, but Sir George could sense the talent that lay behind it. He asked to meet its artist. Carmichael was seventeen at the time.

It was the end of September, the end of the season. When he arrived at the Carmichaels' residence Sir George found almost the entire family sitting around the dinner table; the only missing member was the one he had expressly come to see. Golding offered to lead him to his brother. They came upon him standing in a clearing, hunched over a notebook, a sere wind whipping about him. Sir George stopped in front of him. He was suddenly reminded of Greece's Golden Age. He knew whole pages of Plato's *Banquet* by heart and, later, recited them to Carmichael. He would also show the young man a reproduction of Michelangelo's *Holy Family*. He often said that divine bounty was never better expressed than in the proud body of an adolescent boy. Sir George was a devout Christian, so much so that he had considered joining the clergy, but he was too attached to chastity and celibacy. He would have been absolutely horrified had anyone ascribed to him the impurity of thought he had such difficulty condoning in his precious Socrates. Still, in London, there was talk behind his back—talk that grew louder each time he returned from the countryside with yet another Adonis. But Sir George was innocence itself. He was unsurprised that in the order of things so talented a boy would also be so beautiful. Golding introduced them. As they made their way back to the house, Carmichael permitted the aristocrat to look through his drawing book. What Sir George found transported him. He was now determined to convince the father that the son had talent. (This the father already knew quite well, though he pretended otherwise.) Sir George proposed to purchase, at a very high price, every item in the boy's portfolio, an amount large enough to replace the sails on three mills. The father asked for time to think over this proposal. Sir George departed for his home, having granted the family two days to consider the matter.

Father and son spent those two days quarreling. The father maintained that he would categorically refuse to give his consent. Secretly he hoped that the asking price might rise, for he had never been close to his obstinate, tempestuous oldest son. This turned into one of those long arguments from which there was no return: The son threatened the father, telling him that next season he would make up weather sightings in order to ruin his business. The father retaliated by calling his son a bastard. The son took this to be a figure of speech, but the father, now enraged beyond control, revealed a truth that had been weighing upon his heart for fifteen years. Carmichael was no son of his. The miller had married his mother, with whom he had been madly in love but who felt nothing in return. She was moreover pregnant and would not reveal the name of the father. He was thrown into despair when she died giving birth to the boy. Seeing the beauty of the mother reincarnated in the son tore the elder Carmichael apart. He ended up detesting the child and married another woman to put an end to it all.

On the morning of the second day, the miller let Carmichael depart for the home of the powdered and beribboned old aristocrat—though not before first requiring the boy to sign a pledge, witnessed before a notary, that he would never work for a competitor in the milling business.

From then onward, Carmichael used his mother's maiden name. He moved to London and lived with Sir George. At first, he refused to touch a pencil; he was overwhelmed by the shame of having deigned to draw without first knowing the work of the artists who had preceded him. Sir George had been taking him on visits to friends and associates throughout the capital. Carmichael had seen works by Claude, Cozens, and Girtin—all the greatest painters of the day and of the past, about which their owners spoke reverently to this quiet young man, whose attention to the works was so intense that they occasionally had to pull him away, guiding him toward the salon where dinner was about to be served.

One evening, transported by the heat of a discussion with his protégé, Sir George had one too many glasses of sherry. He led Carmichael to his room to show him an etching he had just purchased, and there he suddenly jammed his hand into the crotch of the young man while uttering obscenities so terrible and sentimental that Carmichael, once he had made it to his own room, believed for a moment that he must have dreamed them. They never spoke of it again. Crushed by horror at what had happened, Sir George resolved to remove Carmichael from his home and gave him a modest income and a sizeable starting sum, so that the young man might find a new address, which Sir George did not wish to know. Carmichael was twenty years old. He would never again see his patron, who died at his family estate in Yorkshire, weakened by the ceaseless penitence he had undertaken for his sins. It had been seven years since their separation.

Without his benefactor, Carmichael no longer had contacts within the world of art, but he didn't care. He decided his apprenticeship was now finished and that he was ready to paint. At the beginning of 1811 he married and moved to Hampstead, into Number 2, Lower Terrace, a small white house set apart from others at the end of a quiet lane. His wife, Mary, suffered from a chest condition and London's air was too foul for her. Spring was ending. The summer of clouds was beginning.

After that mid-summer exaltation, Carmichael launched in a new direction, which was pure painting. These were of course the "skyscapes"—depictions lacking so much as a hint of land, not so much as a treetop or branch to indicate where the sky might end and the earth begin. The sky awaited him each day, always the same and always fresh. The Hampstead Heath was so close to where he lived that all Carmichael had to do to reach it was walk out of his house, cross the garden, and open a small iron gate. Then he headed to the left and turned left again, following a narrow footpath that climbed upward to a crest, and he was there. The entire Heath spread out before Carmichael's feet. He walked in the direction of the Highgate ponds, which lay at the foot of Parliament Hill. He preferred to ascend and descend the hill rather than walk around it because from the tops you could see the docks, St. Paul's cathedral, and the entire city, with its pains and pleasures—and, throughout the week as well as on Sundays, all the humanity that he did not have any interest in painting. At his peak, he produced five skyscapes a day. Though nothing prevented him from finishing ten or even twenty. But five literally exhausted him, and he went home trembling with fatigue and emotion. Mary watched him with concern. Each passing day was taking more out of him. She could see that her husband was being eaten away from within.

Of course, the idea of doing landscapes of the sky hadn't come to him all at once. He first had to grasp that the other things—non-clouds—he was putting onto his canvasses encumbered the clouds. Initially, for example, he always put human figures into the background, where they appeared as a pinkish dab and a few tiny blackish streaks. On the Heath you could find nannies, or farmers returning from the village market. Little by little, Carmichael made them disappear like ghosts into the high grass or at the bases of tall trees, evaporating in either shadow or light. Eventually he stopped painting them altogether. The last figure he did was a woman. At first you can't see her, because she appears in the left-hand edge of the painting, all but dissolved in the bright sunlight. She is holding a parasol made of pigeon-throat silk, whose folds gently echo the green of a flowerless field. If you took three steps back, the figure became indistinguishable from the setting, her water-green dress melting into the verdure, and all the shades of her pale-blue corsage blending seamlessly into the sky. When he had finished that particular work Carmichael knew that he was done with the human figure for good. He saw in this a grand victory—a painter's victory.

From that point on, the only remnant of humanity to remain in his paintings was represented by buildings. He often took up a position against a structure called the Salt Celler because of the shape of its turrets; in the right-hand corner he drew only the line of the tile roof or the edge of a carmine-colored brick wall. Above them loomed the enormous columns of clouds, infinitely mobile, through which the sun's rays poked at irregular intervals. Carmichael crossed one final threshold at the beginning of the month of August in 1812. In a small, nearly square-shaped drawing, the final indication of non-sky is a single wind-shaken branch in the lower right-hand corner. After that, the landscape vanished altogether.

Carmichael was in the habit of pinning his works above the stove in the kitchen. One morning as he prepared to leave, his eye was drawn by one of them. He thought he had never seen it before and yet it seemed familiar. He approached it and held it up, suddenly realizing that it had been hanging upside down. He gave it a quarter turn; yet another painting appeared. How amusing, he thought, and then went on his way. While on the path heading toward the Heath, however, the significance of what had happened began gradually to dawn on him, so that when he reached the top of Parliament Hill, exhausted by the weeks of effort and blinded by his solitude, he believed he had understood its full import: His painting must surpass all others in every manner. He stopped abruptly and headed back down the path toward his house.

Kumo was exhausted by having spoken for so long. Virginie decided she should leave. As politely as she could, she told him that there was someone she needed to meet and that she had to go.

The weeks flew past like clouds before a storm. Virginie did her work with meticulous care, moving through Kumo's collection shelf by shelf, box by box. His, it must be said, was not a true bibliophile's collection. There were almost no rare editions. What made the collection exemplary was that it contained every single work devoted to clouds and more generally to meteorology written over the course of the last three centuries, in every language that Kumo could read— Japanese, German, English, and French. Beginning in the second week of their collaboration, they reversed the schedule: Virginie arrived fairly early in the morning and left after lunch, which most often they ate together at the long table in the library. In the afternoon, Kumo attended to his business, and to whatever his staff and entourage needed of him.

Virginie could see that her employer was in no great hurry. He spent most of their time together telling stories. After awhile Virginie began to understand that these stories, though not exactly fictional, were embellished, sometimes improvised. There were contradictions, such as when he described at length one of Carmichael's works, having said only the day before that none had survived. It didn't matter, Virginie decided. She enjoyed listening to his tales, such as the one about the wise and pious Arab to whom Allah had sent a small cloud to lead him safely out of the desert. Then there was the story of the Templars lost on the steppes of Tashkent, their horses having frozen while crossing a lake. Virginie wondered whether she had fallen in love with her employer. This would be odd, she felt, for she was one of those Westerners who viewed Asians as essentially asexual. Kumo never looked at her with the least hint of concupiscence (a word she liked). Still, she was a little miffed by its total absence.

For quite a long time, Kumo told her, scientists never thought about why the sky was blue. It was of course the same then as now—apparently monochromatic yet consisting of a nearly infinite variety of shades. Thousands of poets wrote about its being azure or cerulean, but not a single scientist bothered to explain why this was so. The poets' evocations were scarcely better than what the scholar-priests offered, for they weren't truly interested in the sky's blueness so much as in turning it into a symbol—the color of eternity from the palette of God. It was as if they couldn't accept the idea that the blue was simply and sublimely of its own creation.

Centuries passed and as science became less a servant of the church the skies were emptied of angels and divinity, filled instead with men in balloons or planes. What came to be understood was that the sky only seemed blue. Explanations followed as to why this was so. The sun has no sense of color; the light it emits is of no color in particular or, rather, all of them. It bombards the earth's atmosphere with light of every wavelength, from red to violet and everything in between—orange, yellow, green, blue, and indigo. But these colors never reach us; as soon as they reach the upper layers of the atmosphere they strike up against tiny air molecules. These air molecules diffract small quantities of light, though not in uniform fashion—they are better at diffusing shorter waves of light than longer ones. That's why the air in the sky won't diffuse red, orange, or yellow light. But it is very good at diffusing blue, and better still at violet. Most of the colors emitted by the sun thus never reach our retinas. That, say scientists, is why the sky is violet. So why does the sky look blue and not violet? Because the eyes of men, even the eyes of men of science, are unable to distinguish violet. We perceive the sky's color as blue just as we sense that the earth is flat or that the sun rises and sets every day.

Increasingly, people—ordinary observers, devoted amateurs, gentlemen farmers—began keeping weather journals, as they were called, in which, day after day, they noted wind direction, the state of the sky in the morning and evening, rainfall amounts, and so forth. The more people shielded themselves from the weather the more they seemed to talk about it, perhaps to pass the time. Meteorologists were persuaded they were on the verge of wresting from the rain and wind all of their innermost secrets. Meteorological societies were formed, congresses convened, and journals published.

These men of science advanced things. Little by little they learned how clouds formed—doing away with a number of even the venerable Luke Howard's own hypotheses on the subject. They had no difficulty getting funding for their research, because their interests intersected perfectly with a seemingly infinite number of financial interests. Steel-hulled ships, very often British and growing in number, were plowing the seas of the world; large office buildings were going up in Geneva and Washington and Berlin and Paris, in which workers used rulers and ink pens to create rectilinear boundaries along what had previously been beautifully round. Empires built to last a thousand years were founded and then disappeared in less than a hundred. More and more people went off to fight and die in distant corners of the world, in villages with strange-sounding names, villages whose existence they had not known of six months before—like Sebastopol or Falluja. The fate of the world depended upon what happened on the seas: It was a war of commerce, as much as war of the more traditional sort. England was in its Golden Age, dealing in spices and rare perfumes, amassing diamonds and opals, constructing white-stoned temples to commerce in its enormous capital city.

Now that the island nation of sailors ruled the universe, weather became a serious matter. On September 5, 1860, the *Times* of London published its first weather announcement. Five years later, on April 30, 1865, Admiral Robert Fitzroy, director of the Meteorological Department at the National Chamber of Commerce, committed suicide because his department had issued an egregiously inaccurate forecast and the press had hounded him for it. As the world was being circumnavigated more and more often, and more and more quickly, it was being learned that climatic phenomena did much the same thing. Simultaneously, it was being learned how high the costs of not understanding the sky and its

movements could prove. The Agriculture Ministry had estimated that the total annual value of agricultural production
worldwide, including horticulture and tree-farming, to be
somewhere around 100 million pounds sterling, and, estimat-
ing that an annual 5 percent growth in productivity would
result from more precise meteorological predictions and
their communication to those concerned (farmers, for example), reliable forecasting had a potential value of 20 million pounds sterling. Simply identifying clouds would no
longer do. One had to predict their movements, their behavior. In 1879, the inhabitants of Dundee and the entire region
were thrilled when a metal bridge was constructed to span
the Bay of Tay, making it no longer necessary to go around
this body of water, reducing travel time to Edinburgh by a
three full hours. Britain's finest engineers had designed the
bridge. Several times a day, heavy iron trains crossed the bridge
without causing so much as a shake. A few journalists specu-
lated about the dangers of conveyance at such high speeds—
close to thirty miles an hour—that would be unleashed upon
the world. In the spring of 1879, after five months of reliable
service, the magnificent new bridge tumbled into the river
whose waters it spanned, taking with it the train that happened to be crossing it and all its passengers. The collapse
was blamed on a series of strong wind gusts that none of the
engineers had been imaginative enough to take into account.
The newspapers were savage in their denunciations. Public
opinion turned sour. A few elected officials tendered their
resignations and, as always in cases such as this, someone took
his life. Several amateur meteorologists wrote memoirs establishing that the architect had not considered wind speeds in

the region. It was decided that a new bridge should be built in the same spot; this one, however, would not collapse.

Despite the occasional setbacks, British technology was unrivaled in the world; at the beginning of that same year, for example, it had permitted Her Majesty's Army to slaughter eight thousand Zulu warriors during the course of several weeks in southern Africa. The Zulus had charged across a plain on foot, spears in their hands, using wooden shields covered with zebra skins, straight into professional soldiers equipped with the finest rifles available. On March 29, 1879, at the Battle of Rorke's Drift, a regiment withstood a siege that endured for several days and killed a thousand native warriors in the process. Those who survived the siege were decorated.

The great and powerful nations of Europe were seeking a way of predicting storms. There were of course always storms, as well as farmers who feared them. But never before had these storms caused quite so many factories to be blown away, or house roofs to be carried off, or cattle and men sent to their doom. In short, never before had so much been at stake. On November 14, 1854, during the Crimean War, a number of warships and commercial vessels—a total of thirty-eight of them, all flying French colors—sank in the middle of Balaklava, in the North Sea. Four hundred souls were lost. Napoleon III summoned the Minister of War, to learn how he could have managed to lose so many lives and an entire fleet, including the mighty three-masted *Henri IV.* In an attempt to save face, the Minister of War in turn summoned the director of the Paris Observatory. The director's name was Urbain Le Verrier. Le Verrier had no difficulty demonstrating to the minister that the evening before it had hit, the storm had been brewing over the Mediterranean, and that two days before this it had been attacking the inhabitants of Europe's northwest regions. A telegram might have averted the whole disaster. Le Verrier was given an audience with the emperor, who wanted to know how such a thing might be accomplished. The director then wrote to every amateur astronomer and meteorologist he could find throughout Europe. Most scientists of the day spent most of their time writing each other about their discoveries anyway. The director's request was straightforward: Could his honored colleagues relay to him their observations about the weather in their regions between November 12 and November 16? He received two hundred and fifty replies, which he posted on a map of Europe in order to track the storm's path. Such a system had a fatal flaw, of course. What good was predicting weather that had already happened? Le Verrier therefore was allocated funds to establish weather stations throughout his native land. The era of individual weather-watching had ended; the moment of the network had arrived. Before long, other countries — Holland, England, Sweden, and Russia — followed France's example.

In August 1996, a decade before meeting Virginie Latour, Akira Kumo celebrated what was supposed to have been his fiftieth birthday. Several months later, he made an odd discovery, which was that he hadn't turned fifty after all. In fact, he had no idea how old he actually was. All he knew was that his birth year was wrong. He found this out completely by chance. A lawyer working for his company decided that for fiscal reasons Kumo should obtain Swiss citizenship. Kumo agreed to the idea. He didn't care about becoming Swiss but had thought about buying some property somewhere high in the Alps, so that he could take morning walks above the cloud line. His staff therefore began to pursue the idea. Among other documents, the Swiss government would require a birth certificate to consider his application. A letter was sent to officials at the Hiroshima city government. A reply came back with surprising rapidity. It regretted to inform Akira Kumo-san that they could not comply with his request, for the city's files had been destroyed in August 1945. Kumo found this confusing. How would the bomb have affected the records of someone born a year after it was dropped? While it was probably due to an innocent mistake, the officials' reply troubled Kumo, and he told his staff that he would see to the matter personally. The weeks passed and slowly, like a sky gradually clouding over, his mood darkened. He wrote to the Hiroshima officials, asking for more information. He felt like someone walking toward a catastrophic event he knows will come but can't quite anticipate. One day in late fall, he got into a taxi and went to the central post office on Rue du Louvre—one of the few in Paris to remain open late—to mail a letter. It was around six in the evening and dark. The taxi pulled up in front of the *poste,* a large gray building. Kumo went in, got his letter weighed and stamped. As he was leaving, the truth struck him: He hadn't been born in 1946; he had been born in 1934. From that moment onward, the tissue of his life started unraveling—not all at once but inexorably.

He had somehow, and with a power that appalled him, managed to erase twelve years of his life. For the first time in decades, he recalled his parents. His father had been a mid-level diplomat, an expert in military affairs. He was exactly the sort of man who might have had reasons to falsify his son's birth certificate—out of the fear that the war would go on forever and that his government was sending increasingly younger soldiers to face the enemy. Kumo knew that this didn't have the ring of truth. Now on the verge of becoming an old man, he was being forced to recollect his memories, a process he found humbling. Thirty years of hard work, thirty years of a career pursued with single-mindedness, stood between him and his childhood. Try as he might, he could remember nothing of his life before Tokyo, nothing before he began studying graphic design. All he had to go on were a few static mental images, like photographs: his mother's quiet elegance; and a shadowy figure always leaving on or returning from some trip—his father. Somehow it came to him that his father had died in Nazi Germany, probably at the Japanese consulate in Hamburg, during an Allied bombing raid in 1945. The image of his mother was inert: quiet elegance, nothing more. It was so sad.

Kumo didn't wait to hear back from the Hiroshima officials. He informed his staff that he would not be applying for Swiss citizenship. The matter was never raised again.

Kumo never recovered from the shock, though somehow he still managed to put together his fashion collections. Time rushed ahead—the spring-summer line was presented and sold and then it was on to the fall-winter line, as every year. But inside he had become stuck in the nebulous mass of those twelve lost years. At moments they seemed as desolate as a field in winter. He hired a private detective agency to find out what they could. In the spring of 1997 the agency presented him with a report that was both clear and precise—yet from which he learned virtually nothing. Under the watchful eye of the occupying American forces, the postwar Japanese government had kept immaculate records. The individual named Akira Kumo was indeed not born in 1946. However, all certitude as to the exact date of his birth had been lost in the chaos at the end of the war. At the start of the summer of 1997, Kumo asked the finest specialists he could find to give him a thorough physical examination, including his teeth. They concluded that he was over seventy years of age. The string kept unraveling, silently, in the labyrinth of his memory.

At the end of July 1997 his fall-winter line was presented. The rehearsals and show had been agonizing; all his models had felt compelled to have nervous breakdowns, having read in the trade magazines that the greatest models regularly did. Business, however, was good—orders were strong. It had been his finest collection ever, said the critics. Kumo, they wrote, had attained the ultimate. His work didn't call attention to itself because it embodied the very essence of elegance.

August arrived and with it the same feeling of boredom and fear Kumo always felt when his staff forced him to take a vacation. He spent two weeks in Amsterdam, and he spent a fortune, going from one woman to the next without really being with any one in particular. His hope was to reach a point of exhaustion, so that he could think of nothing and forget everything. For the first time, however, prostitution seemed to him what it really is: a sordid form of commerce. He felt the sadness of death. On the train back to Paris, while trying to sleep, he suddenly remembered. He had falsified his own records.

After the atom bomb had been dropped, the American army, having taken up a position near the site of the explosion, had required survivors lacking identification to obtain temporary ID cards, which would be used for food distribution. Hiroshima residents who were able made their way to the administration offices, housed in Quonset huts five miles from the point of impact. Among them was Akira. He was already a medical curiosity because he didn't show any symptoms of radiation poisoning. He had been found sitting alone in Zone 2, the area of short-term mortality (in Zone 1 people were incinerated by the blast, and Zone 3 contained those who would die within the year). He didn't suffer from diarrhea, his hair wasn't falling out, his fingers weren't swollen, and he wasn't being attacked by any of several different types of cancer. He agreed to be the subject of tests in exchange for food. American doctors thought about sending him to California for examination. His temporary ID in his pocket, his surplus army bag filled with rations that he had set aside in fear of leaner times ahead, Akira set off for Tokyo. For ten years he lived in the streets. He was sometimes abused; often he ran errands for prostitutes.

In 1959 he learned that the authorities had decided to make the temporary IDs (which the war and postwar periods had generated in huge numbers) permanent. Akira had already spent years surviving by his wits—petty thievery and small-time scams. He was twenty-five but looked fifteen. His youthful appearance had been the source of much teasing. Now he knew that it offered him his best chance for a fresh start. He prepared everything carefully. Told to present himself at one of the offices set up to handle special cases, he chose one located on the outskirts of Tokyo and arrived late in the afternoon. He was made to sit in the hallway on a folding chair. Near him sat the detritus of the Japanese Empire's demise—displaced farmers who had escaped from Russian POW camps on foot; veterans of combat in the Pacific; amputees bearing their Meritorious Conduct in Battle certificates, which they read over and over; widows— some of the many thousands—from across the archipelago. An hour passed, and then another; one by one the folding

chairs emptied. Akira was the second-to-last to be interviewed. As he had hoped, the official who interviewed him—
a young woman—seemed exhausted by the long day's work,
beaten down by the endless procession of misery that had
paraded before her. She greeted Akira politely and without
looking at him told him to sit down, then asked if he had
brought proof of identity. He didn't have any, he replied, because, you see, he had been in Hiroshima on August 6. The
young woman raised her head to look at him. Akira showed
her some medical reports, ones he had chosen with care because none of them provided a date of birth. A good liar
never offers one conclusive piece of evidence; that would be
too obvious. What he does is assemble a raft of little details
that together offer the impression of truth.

Finally the young woman asked his age. The fateful moment had arrived, the one toward which all his efforts over
the preceding weeks had been directed. He was dressed like
a teenager and had given himself a bowl haircut. Starting
weeks before the interview he had massaged his face with oil
twice a day. He spent hours in front of a mirror, practicing
the ways teenagers looked and acted and spoke. He had measured his success toward the end by trying to get in to an
adult-rated film and been refused admission. He had known
he was ready. He told the official that he was sixteen. She
wrote it down without giving him a second glance.

After that, the interview had been a breeze because he
told the truth. He told her about his parents, and how they
had died during the war, forcing him to survive on the streets.
Her responses became more and more maternal. She told
him where to pick up his ID card.

He returned to his former life for a few months. Then he decided what his next move would be. After he had supposedly turned eighteen, he enrolled in a school of graphic design. A new life began, a life that conformed so completely to his desires that the old one vanished, effaced like a child's drawings in the sand by the rising tide.

The train from Amsterdam to Paris reached the Gare du Nord. Kumo's driver had been waiting in front of the train station in his usual spot. Not seeing his boss get off the train, he walked to the nearly empty platform, then onto a car in the First Class section. There he found Kumo, weeping. The driver remembered that Kumo's staff had warned him this happened every August. He knew what to do next. He drove Kumo to the clinic. Kumo continued to weep uncontrollably—not because he was an orphan, or because he had been in Hiroshima, or even because his whole life had been based upon a lie. He cried for having forgotten all of that, for having turned himself into someone capable of forgetting so much. He cried for having survived and because he now understood that he had created his life out of a slagheap.

When he was released from the clinic in September 1997, Kumo went to see a psychoanalyst. He said very little during the sessions—neither did the psychoanalyst—but he knew that talking wasn't the point. The room where they met was quiet and bright. Sometimes Kumo said that he couldn't say anything and very often didn't for twenty or thirty minutes, three times a week. But these silences saved his life. Three times a week Kumo went to the psychoanalyst's office and lay on a kind of flat couch, his head resting on a hard pillow.

There was nothing on the cream-colored walls to look at, aside from a couple of unremarkable lithographs. Light came in from a window that was too high to allow a view, but it did reveal the sky. Kumo started to watch the clouds. Things went on in this fashion—Kumo maintaining his appointment, learning to be patient as he lay on the couch. Finally, Kumo decided that the time had come to emerge from his depression, as if it was something one could decide. The room was empty apart from the analyst, sitting in his chair with his back turned, and the clouds floating by outside the window. He began to speak. He told the psychoanalyst that he intended to collect books on a subject about which he knew nothing but to which he felt attracted. "You see?" replied the psychoanalyst. "You still want to keep things together." His response infuriated Kumo, who told him that he was overpaying him if this little play on words was the best he could come up with. Kumo left, resolving never to come back. Yet there he was at his next appointment, exactly on time, retreating back into silence. A few more silent sessions followed. Then he stopped going.

Officially, he was now sixty-three years of age. The 1997 season was the last one in which he actively participated. After that he became a mere signature. The House of Kumo had been preparing for his retirement for a number of years; two young designers whom he had trained took over the high-fashion end of things. By this point most of the company's income came from accessories—handbags, belts, perfume, and jewelry, though he wouldn't permit them to be mass-produced. Kumo devoted himself to the study of clouds.

He started frequenting the bookstands along the Seine and the rare-book shops in London and Paris. He spent many happy hours looking at the sky from his library, whose shelves began filling with books—rare meteorological tracts, sky atlases, popular books, and scientific tomes that extended to several volumes. He was, he felt, alive again.

On the twenty-sixth day of August in 1883, said Kumo to Virginie, the most powerful explosion the world had known in several thousand years occurred. It happened on the volcanic island—or "Pelean," as we call these islands today, after one such island—of Krakatoa in Indonesia. Pelean islands are volcanic and characterized by a crater capped by a plug, a dome that prevents the lava from escaping; as the dome becomes harder over the years, enormous pressures build up beneath it. Until August 1883, this was the case with Krakatoa. When volcanoes of the Pelean type explode, the dome is shot into the air and comes raining down in a radius as wide as several miles. Sometimes, however, the dome doesn't give way, in which case the entire cone of the volcano sheers off, crushing, burning, and asphyxiating every living thing it passes—be it in air, on land, or in water. Krakatoa was a version of the latter type, the first ever recorded. For years, the gigantic dome at its crown hadn't budged. Toward the end of August the pressures had become so great that the lava found another way out—deep below the water surface. The island, which rose several thousand feet above sea level, was only the visible portion of a mountain that was actually 12,000 feet high. Far below the surface of the water was where the real drama took place. At the foot of the mountain, separated from the freezing water by gigantic plates of rock, a monstrous cone of molten lava trembled. On the 26th of August the lava suddenly opened a breach. In an instant the entire side of the volcano was torn open. Millions of gallons of cold salt water came into contact with millions of tons of molten rock.

The entire island erupted and a gigantic mass of pulverized rock rocketed into the atmosphere, forming the largest cloud ever recorded. In a matter of minutes, the island ceased to exist, vanishing in a towering colossus of gas, dust, and debris. Thus did Krakatoa begin a second life, one that would last for quite some time. With a roar heard for hundreds of miles, the cloud moved out in every direction to begin its assault upon the world.

Though the natives had moved from their fuming island weeks before the explosion, and even abandoned the small chain of neighboring islands, the volcano nonetheless caught up with them. It went on a killing spree, unleashing titanic forces kept bottled up for too long. The first to die were those it found in the immediate vicinity. Some were killed by the noise, which overtook them in a furious wall-like wave moving at 650 feet per second, shattering their eardrums; some died from sheer terror; some were crushed by falling objects of various sorts—boats, trees—which had been swept up from land and sea; others were asphyxiated and burned by toxic gas. The explosion had created a gigantic hole where the island had once been, consuming everything, including the oxygen in the air, creating a vacuum that was hundreds of feet wide. Initially, the ocean had seemed to be suspended around it, as if taken by surprise—the island had been there and now it was not. That soon changed. First there had come earth and fire; now it was the water's turn. From every side and all at once it rushed into the void left by the island, and for an instant what had been a cone of earth and fire became a cone of water. There was a terrifying and brief moment of equilibrium. Then the water began to fall. Though dozens of miles away, the older inhabitants of the area realized what was coming. Flight, they knew, was futile. They offered up their prayers to the gods of the underworld, though those gods seemed not to have survived. Around what had once been Krakatoa gigantic waves rose up, which swept away neighboring islands and engulfed or carried off all boats within a radius of a hundred miles. Two hours later, only a few surviving vessels remained, stranded among the dead fish brought to the water's surface. The carcasses of the other boats were sent spiraling down into the water's dark depths. The most powerful of the waves moved in a westerly direction, a wall of water that reached the top of the sky; it was of such strength that before it eventually petered out in the North Sea, several weeks later, the wave, though much weakened, was still discernable in the channel between England and France.

The water's turn came to an end. The volcano continued to prove lethal through the air. The heated cloud made up of stone pulverized by the explosion didn't dissipate so easily; indeed, it lasted for years. Because of its size it could not be dispersed by the winds, and was itself a storm of dust, water, and wind. First it arched up, reaching a height of ten miles, and for a time seemed to remain immobile; then, a few hours later, like a slow-moving predator, it began to stretch out across the atmosphere, its mass crushing millions of tons of cold air, which, pushing the cloud, sent it spinning slowly into the Northern Hemisphere, altering climates as it went. Everywhere it passed, Krakatoa, now transformed into an unrecognizable giant of water, earth, and fire, lowered the average temperature by several degrees. In the process it caused flooding, brought on an early winter in a number of countries—for several years running—and disrupted the cycles of the seasons. There was a hailstorm in Paris during the summer of 1884. Some saw this as an act of God; others dreamed how weather engineers might turn deserts into gardens. The defunct volcano took a toll on harvests and yields, the growth of certain mushrooms, the reproduction rate of animals, and the health of the very young and very old. It brought ruin, famine, and death. There were those poor anchovy fishermen on the western coast of South America who couldn't locate their catches, which normally formed thrashing schools only a few leagues from shore; the cold currents the fish followed had moved much further off, beyond the reach of the small blue-and-white trawlers. There were the grape growers in the north of Portugal to whom the frosts yielded only slim and late harvests; throughout America there were many miserable souls forced to scratch the hard earth for sustenance, cursing fate and surviving by ingesting roots.

Several years passed, and finally the volcano began to disappear from the sky. At the moment of its death, as if in memory of its glorious past on the earth, the defunct Krakatoa dispersed with gathering speed into every layer of the atmosphere, diffracting the sun's light and producing flaming auroras and magnificent sunsets that seemed like oceans of liquid metal punctuated by emerald green and subtle hints of ocher. No one had ever seen sunsets such as these. The night sky was ultramarine. In London, Paris, and Washington, those devoted to weather anomalies scrupulously noted each nuance; scientists devised hypotheses; poets composed verses. Those in the West well knew that the terrible explosion of a volcano on the far side of the world had altered the seasons, but they did not really know how. Such ignorance was simply not acceptable. They were on the cusp of plumbing the mysteries of atmospheric circulation, cold and warm fronts, and many other things as well.

As for Krakatoa, nothing remained of the island volcano. The waters of the Pacific covered it over; the winds dispersed its cinders to the four corners of the earth; in the earth's core, molten rock groaningly searched for other passages up to the surface. Krakatoa had taken thousands of victims but it did not have the power to destroy humanity. Humanity could only be obliterated through self-destruction. For nature, this marked the beginning of the end.

Virginie could see that Kumo was trying to buy time, putting off finishing the bibliographic inventory. She knew that he was doing this, and he knew that she knew. When neither one felt much like working, a shyness came over them and in a sort of tacit commemoration of their first meeting their conversation returned to the subject which it had all started.

Kumo told Virginie that Luke Howard opposed war at a time when most men dared not, a time when to a profound degree being a man presupposed a love of war. As a Quaker, Howard believed he should translate his opposition into action, and he did so with great courage. He was the contemporary of Napoleon Bonaparte, the greatest military genius and the greatest criminal of the nineteenth century—the hero of the French Revolution and the betrayer of its Republic—and Howard's life span coincided with Europe's most glorious and most hideous conflicts. In 1815, for example, Napoleon's military genius created thousands of orphans and widows across Europe. In the mud of the Waterloo plain, a huge coalition of forces had put an end to the Corsican's activities. The rains, at long last, ceased. The stench of rotting carcasses and gangrenous wounds rose slowly skyward. Their miasmas did little to perturb the French emperor, who was by then fleeing toward Paris, ruminating only upon his fallen fortunes.

The defeat at Waterloo was meteorology's revenge. In 1802, Napoleon had seen fit to publicly dress down an aristocratic scientist, a chevalier, who had come to court to demonstrate his elaborate cloud classification. Napoleon had not understood the point of it—or understood that greatness of spirit sometimes involves accepting things with no immediate practical utility. Worse still, he had made fun of the chevalier and how he described clouds as "veils" and "troops"—or as "dappled," or "broomlike," and "massy." The emperor's lieutenants had laughed along with him. What was the point of attaching names to clouds? They cheered when the scientist left in a huff. The chevalier had learned that the new world order was not much open to serious thought. He never again returned to court.

In June of 1812 Napoleon still mistrusted this new science they were calling "meteorology." A young officer of the Revolution would never have made such a mistake, but an emperor sent six hundred thousand men in the direction of Moscow. A Corsican in temperate France, Napoleon was magnificently indifferent to the weather. His adversary, General Kutuzov, a Russian of ancient lineage, was no such fool. In September 1812, at the battle of Borodin, Kutuzov retreated and abandoned Moscow, which he burned to the ground. He knew that a powerful and indefatigable ally, one that would attack day and night, and by night even more fiercely than by day, would soon come to his aid. The Russian winter was closing in upon them. Napoleon willfully ignored the lesson being offered by the menacing Russian skies. He lingered among Moscow's ruins until October 12, when winter struck. First it killed the starving horses that had shattered their hooves in the frozen ruts. Dying horses were shoved into snow-covered ditches, where they suffered agonies before finally expiring in long shudders. The soldiers ate them and at night took refuge in their still-warm corpses; sometimes, come morning, they, too, failed to awaken. The cold blackened noses and fingers. Men began to fall silently in the snow under the open sky. Others marched on, but winter marched before them. The lucky ones died quickly, dropping onto the road, like a falling pile of sticks. Of the six hundred thousand men Napoleon had dragged into Russia, only half returned unscathed.

And when, on June 18, 1815, it began to rain on the plain of Waterloo, Napoleon still had not grasped the role weather played in military matters. Moscow had apparently taught him nothing. He continued to ignore fate. One last time he hurled thousands of men to their doom. The rumble of battle diminished, the smell of decomposing corpses grew. The Quakers' moment had arrived, the one they had been praying and raising funds for. As soon as relations between England and the continent somewhat stabilized, they went off to help their brothers and sisters.

Howard was among them. One day in July of 1815, while riding on horseback across Belgium's flat terrain, he saw an unusual-looking cloud on the horizon—low, dark, and heavy, it was the only one of its type in the growing twilight. It lay in the direction he happened to be going. By the time he came to within a few thousand yards of the cloud he understood what had created it: The gas being expelled by the cadavers was rising slowly over the hamlet of Waterloo and its environs. Millions of flies droned drunkenly in the evening air; birds fattened themselves upon them. Howard recalled that one of the names of Satan in the Holy Book was Lord of the Flies. That was it exactly. The Devil was here, on the Waterloo plain. Avoiding the guides who were already offering tours of the battlefield, Howard pressed his terrified horse on across terrain that had been tilled by cannonballs and studded with bodies—stripped by pillagers—that had been fermenting in the sun for days. He wandered until late at night toward the northern cities, to which the miserable survivors had dragged themselves, creating so pitiful a spectacle that no one thought to revenge themselves upon these soldiers of the Empire. That evening, before bivouacking in the ruins of a barn, the only one keeping watch over the already forgotten dead, Howard prayed. With all his heart he commended the victims' souls unto the Lord of All Things.

By the end of August, Howard reached The Hague, where he continued to distribute aid to those whose lives the war in its final phase had destroyed. In Haarlem he visited a home for young sinners. Later, back home in London, when recounting the details of his trip, Howard always mentioned one small trip he had made to the Alps, a region proud of its meteorological peculiarities. By this time he had given away all of his funds and distributed among his brothers and sisters all the Bibles his poor beast of burden had carried, and felt he might permit himself a small excursion. He hoped to learn whether it was true that in the mountains some clouds actually remained motionless, perched on a ridge. He arrived in the foothills of the Alps at the end of September and prepared to enter Switzerland. His guides recommended that he walk his horse, which was accustomed to the flat terrain of the Low Countries, up the steep trail to St. Amand's Pass; otherwise it might refuse to move. For an hour Howard progressed along an uneven path through thick fog, following in the footsteps of a guide, who proceeded cautiously. The exertion made his thighs burn. Making one last turn the little party emerged from the fog and out onto a sunny plateau. While his guide unsaddled the horse and gave it something to drink, Howard, as soon as his eyes grew accustomed to the light, turned and looked back. What he saw took his breath. For the first time in his life, he was above the clouds he had spent so much time gazing at. He could barely recognize them. The sky was a sea with waves that lapped gently at his feet. The mountain behind him rose up another three thousand feet; it seemed to Howard like an island paradise. The wind died down, the air was crystalline. Tears came to his eyes; he knelt at the edge of the sky and thanked his Creator. Then he remembered Waterloo. And he thought about his fellow creatures, going on about their business far below him, oblivious to all this grace. So effectively did the clouds muffle their screams of pain and their cries of joy that Howard felt the urge to stay there forever—above both men and clouds. He rose and got back on his horse. Preceded by his guide, he went through the pass and began his descent back into the world.

PART II

Toward Other Latitudes

A cloud is a visible aggregate of minute particles
of water or ice, or both, in the free air. This aggregate
may include larger particles of water or ice and
non-aqueous liquid or solid particles, such as
those present in fumes, smoke, or dust.
—*International Cloud Atlas*

The next morning, neither Virginie nor Kumo were all that anxious to get straight to work. Kumo in particular wanted to drag things out a little, so happy was he simply to see her. Virginie was delighted that she didn't yet have to return to her regular job. They continued to catalogue the works in the collection, but at a leisurely pace, lingering over illustrated plates, chatting about the condition of a certain work or commenting on the signatory of a certain preface. Finally Virginie asked a question about Carmichael. She wanted to know what happened to him.

To tell that story, Kumo replied to her, it was necessary to talk about his marriage with Mary Bickford. Certain references in his journal led one to think that, like Newton, Carmichael had forsworn matters of the flesh to safeguard his genius. He met Mary Bickford three years before they married. What attracted him to her wasn't her looks, for she wasn't beautiful—Carmichael didn't care about such things—but something else. It was that when she entered a room you had to force yourself not to look at her, or to think of things

that were sweet and soft, and yet also to feel a certain sadness. In 1806, Carmichael was in Cornwall with Sir George,
visiting the village of Rosemerryn. To please his benefactor,
who despaired at his charge's blithe atheism, Carmichael
agreed to attend church there on Sunday. To help pass the
time he looked over the congregation and spotted a young
woman, whom he could only see in profile. After the service
he spoke to her, not caring what he said. Her name was Mary
Bickford. She lived with her equally pious and tubercular
brother and parents; she had no dowry. For her part, Mary
fell in love instantly. At a distance, Carmichael followed the
Bickfords all the way to their small farm on the village's outskirts. Three days later, when Sir George was negotiating with
a Rosemerryn sheepherder the purchase of what he thought
to be Roman pottery, Carmichael ducked off, running to the
Bickford farm, where he made his proposal. At first the Bickfords put on a show of friendliness for Sir George's protégé.
They asked him about his prospects. Carmichael, who had
sworn never to lie, told them everything. When he revealed
that he believed in neither God nor the devil the conversation
was ended. Mary was, however, given permission to accompany the young man back. They walked without speaking.
Everything seemed so simple and so obvious to them. He
told her that he had to return to London, but that he would
wait for her. She replied that one day she would come.

Three years later Mary arrived in London. Carmichael
married her without delay in his local parish church. Neither
of them seemed surprised. She was alone now. Tuberculosis
had killed off her parents, as well as her brother. Mary knew
nothing at all about painting. Neither of them was experi-

enced in love. She knew only that the union of their bodies had been blessed by the holy sacrament of marriage. When she had an orgasm she clung to her husband as if drowning. Otherwise she was as happy and serene as a landscape. On Sundays she went to church and prayed for Carmichael's soul, never doubting for an instant that she could save it. Sometimes the minister suggested something about wandering sheep, but these passed her by. She needed nothing and no one. Carmichael had found a mate who never commented on his painting. When he finished a work, she welcomed it the way she would a visitor, with unshakable politeness and confidence.

It was growing late, and Kumo would have to put off telling Virginie the rest of the story until the following day. He knew they would finish the cataloguing of his collection sometime during the course of the week. All that remained were a few boxes, of various sizes. These were the pride of his collection and he had saved them for last. There was a first edition of the sumptuous *Meteorology of the Universe,* published by Teisserenc de Bort, the leading patron of nineteenth-century French meteorology; this copy contained handwritten notations, in French, by the great Danish meteorologist William Svensson Williamsson. In one of the boxes—Kumo could barely contain his excitement at showing it to Virginie—were some of Luke Howard's manuscripts. Acquiring them had been a complex operation: The Society of Friends to which they had been bequeathed courteously but briskly declined to part with them. An American lawyer working for Kumo, someone familiar with Quaker thinking, came up with the perfect solution. In exchange for the manuscripts they would make a sizeable donation to a charitable organization the Friends had founded to promote peace in Northern Ireland. Kumo possessed a signed copy of the short letter Goethe wrote to Howard. It had been acquired in New York along with an original copy of the 1803 lecture, containing the author's emendations, from a half-insane Spanish bibliophile who was passionate about esoteric subjects and who claimed he could prove that Howard had been a Freemason. There were also a dozen or so other less interesting pieces that Kumo had acquired out of principle.

When Virginie returned the next day Kumo presented his treasures to her. She admired them to his satisfaction and they joyfully set to work, side by side, neither needing to look at the other, so intense was their pleasure at being together. Toward the middle of the morning, Kumo picked up where he had left off with the story of Carmichael and Mary. Virginie smiled, then turned and sat in her favorite corner, near the bay window, to listen.

At the beginning of September 1812, a month after he had completed his final sky study, Carmichael believed that at long last he understood what he needed to do. He needed to do thousands of sketches quickly—within the space of a single hour—and then show them in rapid succession to observers. Carmichael had no idea how to accomplish this. He had come squarely up against a wall and was methodically banging his head against it. By the end of September he had stopped painting, convinced that he was on the verge of penetrating to the very heart of clouds' mystery. By now he was fairly insane, of course; Mary was the only thing keeping him attached to the world. He spent entire days on Hampstead Heath, watching the contracting and expanding movements of these masses that he now called "adiabatic clouds"—"adiabatic" referring to the point at which no heat can be gained or lost between a cloud and the surrounding atmosphere. He discovered that the fattest ones grew continuously, seemingly in relation to the heat of the day, and that they retracted at sunset. Therefore, he concluded, only a machine could produce the cloud series, labeling them by hour and by the general atmospheric conditions. Somehow this automaton would succeed in translating information about the tidal movement of clouds—swelling and diminishing—gathered with scientific exactitude, onto a flat surface.

Carmichael was at an impasse. Sir George, who had taken charge of his education, had determined that philosophy—which now might have helped him—would be detrimental to his protégé's artistic development. He was on his own, lacking that friend and concerned colleague who might dissuade him from descending the dark and cold spiral staircase on which he found himself. After a month spent ripping up drawings he had made of his time machine, his head sent spinning by the growing complexity of the October skies over Hampstead, Carmichael was struck by a new revelation. He knew with absolute certainty that chronological and climatic time were one and the same thing. The contractions of the adiabatic clouds were the expression of this periodicity, of the cyclic nature of time, in the same way the seasons are. Cycles, endless cycles. Everything moved and nothing changed. This thought made Carmichael euphoric: What we call "time" isn't chronological but spatial; what we call "death" is merely a transition between different kinds of matter.

He excitedly explained all this to Mary. Neither of them needed to fear death, he said, because the particles that made them up would endure. To the contrary, embracing death opened up new possibilities for life. There could be no shred of doubt that the particles of their two bodies would, one day, be rejoined. Yes of course they would take on very different forms, and probably they would see each without perhaps recognizing one another. But they would never be separated in a universe that was so fundamentally unified. One day, another painter would come along, someone very much like himself, and this painter would uncover the secrets of the sky. Mary listened and smiled.

One day, toward the end of 1812, Carmichael returned from the Heath earlier than usual. He swallowed the remains of the vial that he had just made Mary drink from. For days he had been amassing inflammable products in his small house. He lit a slow-burning wick and lay down next to his wife. He was likely already dead when a gust blew through the kitchen window at 2 Lower Terrace and extinguished the wick, thus keeping the house from exploding in flames. Eventually the smell alerted the neighbors. There were no known descendents. The minister's wife had all their things sold and distributed the money raised from the sale to the village poor. Sir George bought back a sea chest in which Carmichael had thrown his notes and sketch pads. But this old aesthete's confessor was unmerciful. Out of penitence, he had to rid himself of such baggage. Sir George dutifully gave it to a scientist friend, who thanked him effusively and then stuck it in his attic, where it sat for thirty years. The trunk and all that it contained passed from one generation to the next, finally resurfacing in 1997 at a sale in Madrid. Because it contained a first edition of Forster's *Meteorological Research,* Kumo purchased it, and with it, all that remained of Carmichael.

As the summer had worn on, Kumo's stories began getting both shorter and less coherent. They were also getting increasingly sad. This was not really his fault. To help Virginie better understand, he was sticking closely to chronology and thus getting nearer and nearer to the twentieth century, the darkest of them all; at least that's how it felt to Virginie. Kumo didn't seem to notice this. In fact, if anything, he exhibited a sort of nervous excitement while recounting these increasingly dark tales, reveling in the absurdity.

Yet he was waking up at night, panting and sweating, from nightmares. Two were recurring: He was submerged in dark water and just as he managed to reach what he thought was the surface he found not air but more dark water, and the surface of that turned out to be still more dark water, and so forth, endlessly, suffocatingly, for what seemed liked hours but which in the crazy timekeeper that is our mind probably lasted a tenth of a second. In the other recurring nightmare he heard noises in his apartment and knew that men had come to kill him, but he couldn't wake up. At last able to leap out of bed, he ran as far as he could. But the men always caught up with him and calmly cut his throat. Sometimes when he awoke he was standing in some room or in the hall, dazed, humiliated, and exhausted.

At the age of thirty-three, the mathematician Lewis Fry Richardson was named director of the Eskdalemuir Observatory, founded in 1904 in the north of Scotland. Kumo told Virginie this while wiping dust off a file. Richardson was a Quaker. He had never in his life thought seriously about clouds, though without knowing it he happened to be distantly related on his mother's side to Luke Howard. Richard accepted the post, believing that the Scottish climate would suit his wife, Stella, on whom he doted. The year was 1911. During the course of that year, Stella had her seventh miscarriage. No one yet knew about blood types; hers and Lewis's were in fact incompatible. Every evening Lewis prayed that they would have a child. After her fifth miscarriage Stella stopped believing this would happen, but she concealed her doubts from the man she loved; she did not want to cause him pain.

The Eskdalemuir Observatory is located in a desolate place. Both on a month-by-month basis and in terms of total accumulation, the region receives more rainfall than anywhere else in all the United Kingdom. Richardson sometimes wondered whether God had abandoned them, then banished such blasphemy from his mind and focused his thoughts upon his passion—differential equations. Time passed. The summer of 1914 was more beautiful than any in memory, so beautiful that for days on end no rain fell, even at Eskdalemuir. War was declared in Europe, far off to the southeast.

Richardson was a devoted Quaker yet also a loyal subject of the British Empire. He was prepared to be sent to the front and equally prepared to refuse to bear arms. No one asked him his opinion, however. Like all public institutions deemed vital to national interests, the observatory fell under military authority. A well-groomed and deferential colonel took up headquarters in the office adjacent to the director's. The Crown considered Richardson too valuable to be shipped off to slaughter in France. For his part, Richardson thanked God for having placed him at the ends of the earth, able to render service to his country without active fighting. His naïveté was both touching and perturbing, for while he was searching for a peaceful way of making himself useful, millions of men, living and dead, were rotting in the trenches of Marne and the Somme.

Richardson was in the habit of taking long walks beneath the region's turbulent skies; they were an occasion to ponder differential equations. During one of these walks he formulated his calling: He would put his beloved equations to the titanic task of describing the terrestrial atmosphere. And he would very nearly succeed.

As is often the case, the idea formed in his mind in an oblique manner. No serious mathematician would think of applying the relative simplicity of differential equations to the bewildering complexity of climatic phenomena, and Richardson was no different. His solution was therefore to, as it were, rephrase meteorology in scientific terminology by means of a platitude with which everyone is familiar. He did this by dividing up complex equations that might render a numeric prediction of weather in terms of a series of basic calculations.

As with all scientific inventions, all inventions for that matter, it became a question of first seeing it and then getting others to see it. Richardson divided the Earth's globe into quadrants. Within each quadrant were cubes, each with sides measuring around one hundred and twenty miles, for a total of thirty-two hundred cubes; only two thousand of these, he thought, would require calculations, the temperature in the tropical zones being eminently predictable. Then it was a matter of assigning enough "calculators" to each quadrant so that the meteorologist would be given significant warning time—twenty-four hours, for example. He estimated the number of calculators required for each quadrant to be thirty-two. Thus, to get off the ground, Project Organon would require the services of sixty-four individuals capable of making rapid calculations, given that two quadrants were actually involved. While they were out walking in the rain, Richardson told Stella—still not pregnant—about his grand plans. They would erect a building whose inner walls formed a map of the world: On the ceiling would be the North Pole and on the floor Antarctica; on a central tower, a group of calculators would be positioned, each facing their particular quadrant. Within a few hours, the assistant director would carry the first mathematical weather prediction to the director's office, which would consist of a glassed hemisphere atop the Organon's roof. The Organon would issue a thousand dispatches, first to England's four corners, and then throughout Europe, and then across the entire world. These dispatches would save lives by predicting floods and storms, sudden cold spells as well as unexpected thaws.

Richardson published an article describing the Eskdale-muir Organon. It was received with deafening silence. His project was deemed idiotic. It took six weeks before he understood the message that was conveyed by the unresponsiveness of his coworkers at the observatory, and the barely polite acknowledgments from his London colleagues after they'd received copies of the article.

Richardson had established the calculative methods that would be used by several generations of computers. But those computers' existence was years off, and inventing something before it is technically feasible is deemed in the realm of the sciences to be failure. Richardson was perfectly aware of this, nonetheless he was bewildered and disappointed. He abandoned his research. However, God had answered his prayers: At long last Stella was pregnant. Her beauty had always won her a host of admirers. Stella chose the colonel because he was a gentleman and because of all the men at Eskdalemuir he most closely resembled her husband. She had had to endure the colonel's amorous attentions on a number of occasions, but it was worth it. Lewis was radiantly happy. She gave birth to a son. Braced by this unexpected joy, and anxious to restore his scientific reputation by anchoring it in the world of practical matters, Richardson perfected a device that simultaneously measured wind speed and hygrometry, greatly facilitating navigation, particularly in the new field of aviation. For his efforts he received hearty congratulations from both civil and military authorities. Six months after the end of the war, he learned by complete chance why the congratulations had been so vocal. During a pacifist demonstration in London, he met a Captain O'Hara, recently admitted to the Society of Friends. O'Hara had resigned his commission as leader of the first English squadron for aerial reconnaissance.

Richardson didn't know who O'Hara was but O'Hara knew who Richardson was, and told him why. During the last two years of the war, Richardson's anemo-hygrometer had given British aviation a huge boost because it had resolved a complex problem involving the use of toxic gasses. The army had employed it to distribute the gas, whose efficacy depended upon wind direction and humidity levels in the air; released at the ideal spot, it would spread out uniformly in all directions, from a zone of between zero to fifteen feet, leaving no enemy combatant with a chance of survival. Richardson's device had played a decisive role in the victory. He never invented anything again.

The first computer was created in 1946. A few years after that, one of these new machines, a model known as the ENIAC, was put to the task of calculating weather predictions. The operation took place in Maryland. After he heard about it, and without the least bitterness, Richardson immediately wrote his colleague John von Neumann to offer his congratulations. There is no record of a reply. During the 1920s, Richardson, who had resigned from all of his research positions, attended a lecture given by Edwin Schrödinger, one of the fathers of modern physics. Schrödinger had developed a brilliantly generalist approach, one which Richardson found very odd. Schrödinger termed this approach "holistic" and it offered abstract notions, such as the idea that a cloud was a completely impenetrable black box that might be understood as going from state A during weather T, to a state B in $T + 1$. Although he recognized in this his old way of thinking, Richardson concluded sadly that he would never understand the purely mathematical approach of his young colleague. He felt old; he was all of sixty. At a cocktail reception at the bar of the Strand Hotel given after his presentation, Schrödinger learned that Richardson had attended his lecture and asked to shake the hand of the man who had shown the way. They looked everywhere for Richardson but couldn't find him.

Richardson spent the rest of his life attempting to create a mathematical model for the reasons certain human groups wage war. He died, secure in the affection of his wife and three children. No one ever followed up on his final project.

Just as Akira Kumo realized that soon he would have nothing more to recount to Virginie, a call came from London, informing him that Abigail Abercrombie was dying.

All great collections tend to orbit around a missing piece, a central absence that acts like a hub around which revolve, indefinitely, the collector's desires. The piece in question might have been lost ages earlier, or it might exist but its present owner adamantly refuses all offers. In the case of Kumo's collection, the missing piece bore a name, a name celebrated in meteorological circles: *The Abercrombie Protocol.* The only known copy of it belonged to its author's daughter, Abigail, and no one, so far as it was known, had been allowed to inspect it. Therein lay the *Protocol's* utter originality. It was famous because no one had seen it. Like other interested parties, Kumo had only the official bibliographic description to go by. The description had been done in 1941 and was fairly limited in scope. *The Abercrombie Protocol* was a thick volume, its dimensions forty by fifty centimeters; it was covered in textured bottle-green cardboard and bore only its title; it had a ring binding, and the rings, six in all, were made from nonoxidizing steel; it consisted of 732 pages, each numbered in Arabic numerals in violet ink; a substantial number—the exact number was unknown—of illustrations; and handwritten text of varying length; the text and illustrations extended to 517 pages; the other pages were pristine; it was in perfect condition, aside from two small water stains on the spine. There ended the bibliographic description.

The Abercrombie Protocol was the greatest mystery of the meteo-bibliographical world. Only three people had presumably read it: the author himself (if an author can be said to "read" his own work); his adoptive daughter, Abigail, who consistently refused to reveal anything about it; and Abigail's son, Richard Abercrombie, Jr. Richard Abercrombie, Sr., died in 1917. His *Times* obituary, though brief, offered proof enough that in his day Abercrombie was a notable personage. A wide variety of scientific organizations from around the world offered written expression of their condolences. But no one had ever managed to engage Abigail Abercrombie even in preliminary negotiations over letting go of the book. And now she was dying on the sixth floor of Whittington Hospital. Kumo didn't think for a second that this notoriously prickly and eccentric old crone would be persuaded to sell the *Protocol* simply because she was on the verge of death. Nonetheless, her dying offered him a way of buying some time.

Kumo explained the situation to Virginie. For years Abigail Abercrombie had refused even to meet with agents acting on behalf of potential buyers, whether individuals or institutions. What made her refusal so curious was that she was widely known to be avaricious. She had sold off her father's possessions to the highest bidder right after his death: original manuscripts of articles that appeared in *Meteorological Journal;* his correspondence with the greatest names in the field; his collection of watercolors, including significant works by Boudin and Constable. These were scattered to the four corners of the world, despite good-faith and even generous offers made by the British government to keep them at home. Abigail would entertain no discussion about selling the *Protocol,* however. Kumo had never explicitly made his case to her, at least under his own name. Abigail Abercrombie was known to consider non-Caucasians subhuman.

Kumo offered Virginie a mission: to go to London, meet with Abigail or Richard Abercrombie, or both, and find out where matters now stood.

The private detective agency Kumo had hired to keep an eye on Abigail proved worthy of its reputation. The blue folder Virginie was handed at the train station was impressively thorough. While en route to London, she wondered what she could possibly say to a dying woman she had never met to persuade her to sell her father's book. The folder contained what was thought to be the most recent photograph of Abigail, taken with a telephoto lens. She seemed to be looking straight at the photographer, appeared to be around seventy years old, and conformed to the stereotypical image of a witch. Virginie wasn't overly concerned. Her chances of success were slim. But this was a free trip to London. She was looking forward to practicing her English.

Highgate is a lovely residential area inhabited by surgeons, rock stars, and prosperous dealers of six-month-old Indonesian antiquities; in other words, the sort of wealthy

people who like to pretend they lead simple lives among ordinary people. Perhaps to save money, Abigail had chosen to
be treated in Whittington, which was a public hospital. Virginie arrived, feeling quite pleased with herself for having
followed the conversational patter of her taxi driver, who was
from the north of England. She was equally able to understand the directions given to her by a nurse, a dark-skinned
young man with a thick East End accent, and before she
knew it she was on the sixth floor of Whittington Hospital
and standing outside Room 64. She knocked, opened the
door. The room was bright and clean but depressingly devoid
of furniture. No one was there. She stepped back into the
hall. A gurney was pushed up against the wall on the left, and
lying on it was a body covered with a plastic sheet, softening
the contours of what lay beneath. The body was so tiny that
it could have been a child's. Virginie lifted the sheet and
peered under. The old woman was recognizable. She didn't
look mean or unkind. Her eyes, wide open, were filmed over
and dried out, staring straight at the drop-panel ceiling. She
gave off a slight smell.

A voice behind her spoke, making Virginie jump, though
the voice was gentle and not intended to startle her.

Kumo was more than tired, he was drained. When you're merely tired you sleep or take some vitamins, maybe spend an hour in an oxygen tent. He was like an evaporating pool of water with no source refreshing it, and he knew that as time passed he would gradually and relentlessly continue to diminish. He had always been an awkward conversationalist. At first, interviewers complained about his laconic manner, then decided how really marvelously Japanese it was. Hiring Virginie had given him some extra days. Now she was gone. Kumo was too exhausted even to think about what came next. Of course all he had to do was tell her he wanted her to be with him for a portion of each day; she would, he knew, agree without hesitation. It would be so much simpler, just as things could always be so much simpler than they were, except that there are so few people able to achieve such simplicity. Rather than call her, he went to his desk. He hadn't written a letter in years. For nearly the first time in his life, Kumo was sitting down to write a letter to a…friend. The people he'd been closest to were those for whose services he

paid—employees and prostitutes—and to his mind the connection between a word and what it signified had always
been unimaginably rich. "Friend." He almost didn't know
how to begin.

The reason that the body of the woman who had died in
Room 64 at Whittington Hospital had been rolled into the
corridor was so that the room could be prepared for the next
occupant. The man whose voice had made Virginie jump approached her. He was a little heavy but one of those people
you would never imagine as thin. His age was indeterminate—he might have been fifty, give or take ten years. He
politely repeated the question he had asked, given that the
young woman seemed not to have heard him: Had she known
his mother? Virginie couldn't reply either yes or no and instead decided to explain why she had come. The man told her
that the *Protocol* wasn't for sale. Virginie couldn't tell whether
he felt apologetic that this was the case. He never seemed to
stop smiling.

There was nothing more for Virginie to do. The Pak-
istani nurse who earlier had directed her to Room 64 now
approached the man, a suitably solemn expression on his
face. He told him about the old woman's final moments.
Out of kindness he neglected to mention the insults she had
heaped upon him right up until her final breath. Virginie took
advantage of the moment to walk away from them down the
hall. As she walked she heard the man's voice again, calling to
her. They rode the elevator down together. He told her that
he wasn't upset in the slightest that she had come about the
Protocol. It was simply that his mother had sold so many things

belonging to his grandfather that he couldn't bear to part
with this one thing. He also told her that his mother's burial
would be the day after tomorrow, at half past eight in the
morning. Feeling as if it might make up for barging in upon
his life, Virginie told the man that she would attend. She jotted down the address he gave her and left.

Virginie watched television in her hotel room all afternoon; she didn't have as many channels at home. Then she
called Kumo's number. He was at a meeting and not to be
disturbed, she was told. The best thing would be for her to
stay on in London a little longer and await further instructions. Virginie was content to do that. For two days she
walked the streets of her favorite city in the world; she particularly loved the winding lanes in Soho. She went to a museum she'd never been to before. In the evening she stroked
herself in the bathtub, afraid that if she did it in the bed she
might stain the mattress, and then fell asleep with the TV on.
The morning of the burial, a Friday, she left very early so as
not to be late.

The address Richard Abercrombie had given her was in
Highgate Cemetery, located directly behind Whittington
Hospital. The cemetery, divided into an eastern and western
section by Swains Lane, seemed completely deserted at this
hour. It was bordered by high walls belonging to adjoining
private residences that were topped with barbed wire and
surveillance cameras. A taxi dropped Virginie near the cemetery's western section; a caretaker she came upon told her
that she should cross to the eastern section. She passed beneath the main gate, which she found fairly hideous, the kind
of fake medieval architecture built in homage to the works of

Walter Scott. She came upon another caretaker, who looked as if he might be the twin of the first, and he offered to show her the way. They walked up the main alley. The cemetery had been used as a backdrop for so many horror films, videos, and shampoo ads that it gave first-time visitors the feeling of déjà vu. Its western section had known its greatest moment at the end of the nineteenth century, when dying had been an integral part of society life and it had been *the* place to be buried, perhaps because it seemed to fulfill a profoundly British fantasy: that of being buried in the countryside while still in the heart of London. Highgate had the feel of an aban-doned park. The phony Gothic quality seemed less distract-ing the deeper into it you went, and the more compelling the smell of humus and dirt that rose up from among the under-brush and tombs. Everywhere you looked—along the mossy walkways, in the gaps in the thickets, in the grassy hollows—were friezes of portly cherubs sporting with deer and lichen-ravaged Madonnas. The cemetery's intense beauty worked on Virginie, to the point that she could imagine how won-derful being buried here would be, how wonderful to decom-pose among the dead leaves and overgrown brush. She walked in silence directly behind the caretaker, who was puffing; the path, though straight, was steep and uneven. The day prom-ised to be hot, though right at this moment the temperature was perfect and the air eveninglike in its calm.

The caretaker stopped before a sort of plateau, from which three paths branched off. He indicated to Virginie that she should take the one on the right, and then he turned and went back down the hill. A little way along the path she came to a grassy clearing. Richard Abercrombie was already

there, standing with his back to her. He faced a small casket
sitting on a trestle in the shade; his hands were in his pockets. He was looking away to the south. He wore a dark suit,
which made him seem older, Virginie noted. He might be as
old as sixty. Out of breath, and concerned that she'd arrived
too early, she was preparing to say something appropriate
when Abercrombie, having heard her approach, turned and
smiled, and then with a sweep of his arm indicated what he
had been gazing at. Virginie gasped. The entire city of London was spread out at their feet in the morning sun. They regarded the view without speaking. Virginie didn't try to pick
out particular landmarks; she let the full extent of the vista
overpower her. It was half past eight in the morning. Four
cemetery workers were standing discreetly at the edge of the
clearing and talking in hushed tones. For no particular reason they decided to wait another half hour, though Abercrombie informed them that he doubted anyone else would
turn up. He had placed an announcement of his mother's
death and burial in the national newspapers but received
no confirmations of attendance. While they waited, he proposed to Virginie that they walk a bit. Smiling, as ever, he
explained that only those families with a concession dating
back to 1895 had the right to be buried in Highgate. Such
was the case with the respectable branch of the Abercrombie clan, though these aristocrats would never seriously have
considered being buried anywhere other than on their Scottish properties. The Highgate concession had thus remained
empty. It would have been the perfect resting place for his
mother, had she not stubbornly reiterated her formal refusal
to be put there.

Abigail had wished, instead, to be cremated. The four cemetery employees, followed by a cortege of two individuals, climbed toward an Egyptian-style structure made of reinforced concrete that housed the crematorium and hundreds of urns. The idea had been to create a sort of truncated pyramid, except that, half-buried in the earth, it looked more like the bunkers the Germans had constructed along the coast of France during the war. They descended into the crypt. Abercrombie and Virginie sat before the open door of the oven, while the workers went about their business. Virginie thought it was time that she offer her condolences, and did. This had the effect of making her companion laugh out loud. The employees took no notice; they had seen nearly everything in their line of work. But it did upset Virginie, who thought she must have made some terrible mistake in her English. Someone shut the oven door, through which you could catch a last glimpse of the white casket. Abercrombie was asked to light an imitation log. He did so and sat back down. He asked Virginie if she knew anything about cremation. She replied she didn't. It would take two hours, and he was very sorry indeed to have upset her just now. It's just that had she known his mother she would never have offered her condolences. Abigail Abercrombie was not one of those whose loss was cause for sorrow. Moreover, had Virginie known his mother, she most certainly wouldn't have come to her cremation. He offered to tell her a little about Abigail Abercrombie, both to pass the time and as a way of thanking her for making the effort. Only if she was interested, he added. Virginie of course said that she was.

As she might have surmised, the Abercrombies were more than a family, the Abercrombies were a *name*. The clan had long been closely associated with Scottish history and with some of the grander moments of the British Empire, to which it regularly furnished heroic generals, dedicated scholars, pious archbishops, and extraordinary women. Until 1889, Richard Abercrombie promised to be one of those dedicated scholars. But everything unraveled in the later years of his life, shameful ones so far as his family was concerned. He neither married nor produced offspring; he died in 1917 at the age of seventy-five. But in 1912, to the chagrin even of his most loyal servants, who sensed that their lifelong devotion to him might translate into being named in his will, Abercrombie had adopted a little girl, an orphan of unknown parentage to whom he gave the name Abigail and raised as his own. The family briefly hoped the child might actually be his; the truth was the little girl didn't carry a drop of Abercrombie blood in her veins.

His adoption of this commoner created a sensation in London society; it was even spoken of in the House of Lords, where Abercrombie's younger brother had a seat. Nonetheless the family's black sheep seemed unmoved by the scandal he had created. He also anticipated his family's next step and consulted with the finest barristers he knew. Abigail Abercrombie would not be disinherited. At Richard's death one of his servants, actually in the employ of the deceased's brother, quietly burned two copies of the wills before the medical authorities had arrived. Success was short-lived. A notary public in Dublin presented himself soon after he had read about Abercrombie's death in the *Times;* he was in possession of a copy of the will, as were several of his colleagues in Dundee, Liverpool, and Lincoln. Each and every one was signed and each and every one contained identical provisions. The terms of Richard Abercrombie's final wishes were straightforward and legally binding. Abigail would inherit his estate when she turned eighteen, and his oldest and most incorruptible servant would act as her guardian. Immediately, the Abercrombies announced they would challenge the will in court, as a matter of course, but bided their time, hoping that the scandal would simply fade. The years passed.

By the time Abigail approached her majority, her wayward behavior became a comfort to the Abercrombie clan, for it reinforced their notions of bloodlines. Not only was the young woman a commoner, she was a particularly shrewd one; and she revealed a capacity for vulgarity that was all the more remarkable given the superb education she had been given in an attempt to compensate for her inferior breeding. The family now understood that it was no longer a question of erasing the stain her adoption had made on the family's name; it was, instead, a matter of ensuring that this stain spread no further. Thank God the creature expressed her baseness in the same manner as did others of her class: money.

In 1934, Abigail, whose existence now threatened to sully the family name in ways they had never thought possible, lost no time in contacting the family she had never set eyes upon. The family quickly agreed to negotiation, particularly as it had learned that she was shacked up in her father's house in Kensington with a garage mechanic. Thus began an unending series of payments: The clan paid for Abigail to travel to the continent, on the express condition that she take her young man with her, and therefore remove herself as far from London and its echo chambers as possible; it paid off the garage mechanic when he left Abigail and threatened to write an account of their life together for the newspapers; it paid the young man who replaced the garage mechanic in her affections, a one-time sailor without other employment, and a drunk as well, in order to keep his excesses as quiet as possible. After twenty years of being extorted the Abercrombies began to realize the extent of their naïveté: Abigail would never renounce the name she carried.

This fact was dawning on them when an unforeseen event threw them even further into despair. At the age of thirty-nine, Abigail discovered that she was pregnant. She had thought herself infertile and this had not displeased her, for it meant she could submit to the amorous advances of her lovers without consequence. The doctors suggested to her that she have an abortion—after all, they told her, she was almost forty years old, of questionable physical condition, and had a checkered history. The child would be an imbecile and probably violent.

He was born in 1946. The father was unknown. Contrary to all expectations, Abigail settled down. She became somewhat interested in religion; she planned a brilliant career for her son; she retreated to the Kensington home. Richard Abercrombie was raised according to the very strictest principles by a watchful mother who made no attempt to conceal her past, and by an army of private tutors.

———

An employee approached to announce that the crematory process was complete. Abercrombie gave them his address for delivery of the ashes. You couldn't simply cart them off, he noted to Virginie. The ashes needed to cool. Bodies are actually quite durable; sometimes it was necessary to put them back into the oven to reduce them to the powder that corresponds to our notion of what a dead person's ashes should look like. Virginie and Richard ambled back through the clearing, lingering silently before the view in the hot sun, and then headed toward London.

Abercrombie smiled as he spoke to her in the shadow of the main gate. He was one of those men who could speak without needing a reply. He had determined from the very first that he would sleep with Virginie. She was not exactly pretty, but he found she aroused him sufficiently. She would be his first post-freedom mistress. At fifty-nine, Abercrombie had recently liberated himself from the woman he had married at thirty, and to whom he had been unfaithful almost from the start. For nearly thirty years she had been suffering and bemoaning his frightful egotism without leaving him or doing anything about it. Enduring marriage with him seemed better than a life of solitude; besides, one had to accept one's lot in life. Finally, however, she did leave him.

Virginie found him charming. She wondered whether she had fallen in love with this man. She was sorry to wonder about this so early on; it was too late for things to simply…happen. She was in love, she decided. Even if untrue, it was such a pleasant thought. Abercrombie invited her to his home for dinner that very evening, without bothering to give the impression that all he really had in mind was dinner. She accepted, knowing that he knew that she knew. They walked to the end of the shady avenue that bisected the cemetery. Virginie found a taxi. Richard went home on foot to clean up the house, do a little shopping, and have a nap.

Back at her hotel Virginie studied her map of London and saw that Richard Abercrombie lived mere steps away from Hampstead Heath. It was a sign, she told herself. She liked believing in signs when she was in love, even when only a little in love. All afternoon she dreamily prepared herself for the evening. Twenty-five minutes after she had left the hotel, a messenger dropped off a thick red-and-blue envelope. Inside were a dozen sheets of royal-sized paper, folded in half, numbered in Arabic numerals in the upper right-hand corner, and covered in an oversized, childish scrawl. Toward six o'clock Virginie emerged from a taxi at 22 Willow Street; she was depilated, perfumed, carefully coiffed and dressed, and generally aroused. A plaque next to the front door informed her that Abercrombie was a psychoanalyst. The house's façade was unremarkable—three-story brick with a flat roof and three windows facing the street, like practically every other London townhouse. The interior was a different story. It was gorgeously decorated, so much so that several design magazines had done articles on the sitting room and library attached to Dr. Abercrombie's private office. He had welcomed the attention. They had sent some young female staff writer who ended up fellating Abercrombie on the priceless Afghan carpet on the top floor, in the bedroom, the highpoint of the visit because of its Victorian nightstands (which were in pristine condition) as well as its view of the Heath.

Abercrombie received his patients between eight in the morning and eight in the evening, six days a week. He had taken two days off for his mother's burial, the first days he had taken off in five years, not counting Sundays, which he usually spent tinkering and hunting for antiques. Apart from that, Abercrombie did nothing except have sex. The hours of inactivity he spent waiting for Virginie were a novelty to him and made him tipsy. When Virginie rang at the front door he didn't even bother to offer her a tour of the house. They kissed immediately in the entryway. They made it to the sitting room. She was lying on the couch in the twilight. He was on his knees before her, touching her sex with his fingers and his tongue. It was his fingers that left her gasping, for he touched her exactly as she touched herself. She had not recovered from her surprise at this when suddenly her orgasm overwhelmed her. Feeling the moisture under her thighs she reddened in the half-light. Abercrombie seemed to take no notice of the puddle. He calmly wiped his fingers on a cushion. He had planned to replace the couch anyway. They took a break to nibble on some hors d'oeuvres and have a drink. She apologized for what had happened. He resisted telling her that he had seen the phenomenon before—he and his couch—and went off to prepare. Before he left he settled her at his computer so that she could do some research on the Internet. Her form of orgasm turned out to be rare but it did have a name; there were even some DVDs you could buy. Virginie was disappointed. She had secretly been proud of her voluminous secretions, and yet this thoughtful man seemed so nonchalant about them. She went into the kitchen and pushed him up against the sink. It was her turn. His sperm tasted salty rather than sweet.

The day that followed resembled the one before: They spent it in bed touching each other. They played and came and slept, without talking. The weather was wild—rain slashed against the windows on Willow Street, storm clouds moving from east to west. The urn was delivered, and at around five in the evening Virginie and Richard went for a walk, to give their muscles a rest though it was cold and raw. They walked all the way to the southern border of the Heath, climbing a small hill that overlooks a long, narrow pond. It was still raining, but lightly. Richard took a small coffee-tin-sized container out of his pocket and looked around for a secluded spot. Off to the side of the path he found a small depression. Opening the small container he poured its contents onto the wet grass. The remains of Abigail Abercrombie were spattered with raindrops, turning into a darkish clump that gradually leached into the ground. Her express wish, communicated to her son two days before her death, was that her remains not sit around in some dump for urns. He must see that they didn't. Richard had done so, and to his enormous surprise he suddenly felt great sadness. Tears formed in his eyes. He thought about his childhood, and the feeling immediately dissipated. Together he and Virginie walked back down the hill, huddled under the same umbrella. He tossed the container into a rubbish bin.

They went back to his house on Willow Street. Richard went straight to his library, and from a drawer in a cabinet built beneath one of the bookshelves pulled out a metal box.

Inside it was a large, overstuffed green notebook that resembled a photograph album. He opened it and flipped
through it, searching for something. Locating the page he
sought, he placed the book on Virginie's knees. A black-and-
white photograph had been glued to the right-hand side
of the page with little adhesive corners made of crystalline
paper. It looked at first glance like any other old photograph.
It was of a naked woman, taken from below her knees. She
was looking at the camera, wearing no jewelry, and her pubic
hair had been shaved off. The image was of exceptional clarity. You could make out small razor burns in the milky folds
where the skin is most sensitive. Her breasts were high, and
she seemed Asian. With her right hand she was spreading
apart the folds of her sex.

Virginie was struck by how stunning the woman was, and
how matter-of-fact. Oddly, the photograph didn't seem pornographic, not even particularly vulgar. She said this to Richard,
who was sitting next to her. He agreed. And yet, she added, it
was very arousing, unquestionably arousing. Again he agreed.
She placed *The Abercrombie Protocol* on the coffee table and
undid his zipper and his belt. She and Richard closed their
eyes from pleasure.

The letter from Kumo was waiting for Virginie at her hotel.

In order to talk about my childhood, he had written, I have to start at the age of six or seven. The war was coming to an end, slowly but surely, among the thousands of islands that made up what was called the Pacific Theatre. They say that the endings of wars are the worst because they don't ever really end. Each day that drags past should have been the first day of peace. This would be one of those wars that ended too late, even for the victors. The losses would be staggering. The Americans were progressing island by island, each more nightmarish than the one before. They landed before day-break on a beach bordering a jungle that was pockmarked by bombardment, which had gone on all night long and yet still left it essentially unchanged, still dense, and obstinately, inhumanly impenetrable. The Marines sprinted across the beach in the direction of the jungle, from which an unseen enemy fired with deadly accuracy at the silhouettes outlined so clearly against the beach. Even when the beachhead was narrow it was still D-Day all over again, except that it went on day after day, an archipelago of bloody battles, each one fought on terrain that was uninhabited and uninhabitable even in the best of times, but which, because of location, had been transformed into a priceless commodity. When the Marines reached the jungle and took refuge behind the first trees, they found it deserted. The Japanese soldiers had retreated to the interior. The Americans fired mortars from the beach. The ships offshore shelled the terrain ahead of them. Finally they began to advance, because Americans were always advancing, dying in droves but undaunted—and always, always advancing.

The fighting between the Americans and the Japanese was without precedent. Even at Pearl Harbor they hadn't seen each other from close-up. There is something almost insane about countries without common borders going to war, something unnatural. The conclusion of this war would not be like any other. For one thing, the Japanese army had pulled back, like any army in any war when it finds itself out-manned and outgunned. The difference is that the Japanese didn't retreat to regroup their forces and prepare for a coun-terattack; nor, indeed, in order to save their skins. They had long since accepted the idea that this war would have no end. They had known from the beginning they would lose it, and they were losing it. No, they pulled back as a way of prolong-ing the losing for as long as possible, to entice more and more of these healthy, well-fed enemy combatants from across the sea into sacrificing their lives. They were seeking a simple calculus: The number of deaths among the victors must equal the number of deaths among the vanquished, so that, when it was all over, telling which was which would not be easy.

The Japanese took it for granted that their empire would collapse and that not one of them would survive. What remained to them was spoiling the victory. Of all the world's civilizations, America was the one that most needed losers. It needed a Japan and a Germany and an Italy forced into submission and a France and a Belgium on their knees. It needed these things like a loving but demented child dreams of his parents being brought low, so that he might feed them and put them back on their feet and loan them money and tell them what to do. From this point of view, things were going well in Europe. There, everything was falling into place. Eventually, the same thing would happen in Japan. But right at this moment, in the Pacific Theatre, the horror went on and on and on. Wounded Japanese soldiers booby-trapped their bodies with grenades that went off. American authorities gave orders that no one was to touch the bodies of Japanese soldiers. They learned to dispatch the wounded from a distance. They shot anyone who surrendered, for the same reason. On those few islands with a civilian population, the women threw themselves without complaint from the tops of cliffs, clutching children in their arms. Those who witnessed this sight would never forget the dull wet thud of flesh and bone striking rock.

Slowly the American army tightened its hold and trapped the final resistors—against a wooded hillside or in some valley that hadn't appeared on the maps. Here they came up against one final obstacle, for the Japanese had foreseen such an eventuality and booby-trapped the underground tunnels they had built. Every twist and turn in these tunnels took American lives. Whenever they could, the Marines called in the flamethrowers. Before they did that they first were careful to secure the area; the last thing they wanted was for the flamethrowers to get picked off. Flame-throwing equipment isn't all that complicated; anyone can learn to use one in an hour. What was rare was finding men capable of coming to within feet of those they would burn alive, men who were capable of looking at faces blank with terror and still shoot the flame. Such men were valuable, and sought after by every unit in the Pacific Theatre.

At the end of July 1945, the American commanders estimated that twelve hundred soldiers per day would lose their lives on these Pacific islands. This was a higher number than anticipated. It was also beyond what American public opinion would tolerate, particularly now that Europe had been brought more or less under control. The estimates of the number of wounded—far greater than the number of those killed—were even more worrisome from a military standpoint, for the wounded posed greater logistical challenges. One dead body required two men either to bury it or to transport it to the rear. A wounded soldier, on the other hand, immobilized five men for an indeterminate amount of time; and who knew whether it was even worth the effort. By the end of July 1945, a conclusion had been reached: The war in the Pacific needed to be over.

On a military base in New Mexico, thousands of miles from Japan, the final preparations for the Manhattan Project, which had been started years earlier, were underway. The project had brought together the finest scientists from America and Europe. Among them were a number of Jewish physicists eager to be involved in something that, they were told, would help destroy the man who had chased them from their homes and murdered their families. They worked with passion. They worked even faster when they heard about the V1 and V2 rockets Hitler was preparing to launch. The greatest worry was that these missiles might carry the Ultimate Weapon. In the end, however, the Allies got it first. Never before had a weapon of such awesome power been invented in so short a time. By 1944 it was considered operational. The American military command expressed its gratitude to the team, and then immediately turned to the question of whether to use it on Japan. Using it against Germany was never an option. The scientists, Jewish and gentile alike, were extremely disappointed.

By July 1945, the bomb was ready to go and the targets established. The decision to use it came after adherance to all the procedures required by a modern democracy. First a steering committee, consisting of civil authorities and military men, selected a list of sites: Kyoto, Nagasaki, Niigata, Kokura, and Hiroshima. One of the civil authorities had been upset that Kyoto, which had so many historic monuments, was on the list; it was taken off. The list was then transmitted to the air force. The target would be chosen at the last minute and be determined by logistics. The technical teams assigned to evaluate the effects of an atomic bomb on an urban target made a special request to the military chief of staff. They hoped that the target would be a city that had not already been bombed by traditional means and therefore be intact, so that they could more accurately measure the degree of devastation. Until the beginning of August 1945, the populations of Kokura, Niigata, Nagasaki, and Hiroshima had considered themselves fortunate; no American bomber had flown over them. The teams made another request: They would prefer that the target be situated in a river valley. That way, the shock wave produced by the bomb would be easier to track. The military command had no objection to either request.

Have you never wondered, wrote Kumo to Virginie, why two bombs were dropped on Japan in 1945? Why Hiroshima first and then Nagasaki? Why was one bomb dropped on August 6 and another on August 9? Why not just one? It is a question that no one seems to ask, except perhaps children learning for the first time about what happened. The answer is that the Americans had invented two kinds of atomic bombs and they needed two different sites to try them out.

On August 6, 1945, around seven in the morning, an American reconnaissance plane flew over Kokura, Niigate, and Hiroshima. No one living in the first two cities heard the little plane—the cloud cover was thick and low—and hence there was no panic. When it flew over Hiroshima at 7:15, the skies had cleared and the wind had died down. Those inhabitants who were up and about could see the plane. Again, though, no one panicked. It wasn't a bomber. Moreover this was the third time in three days that this small plane had appeared and then disappeared, and it had never been followed by heavy bombers, as some had first feared. The city authorities were early risers and watched the small plane pass over their city. Their thoughts turned to their less fortunate fellow citizens living along the coast. So many lives had been lost in this war. They had stopped believing in the radio broadcasts announcing certain victory. The little plane soon vanished, its hum growing fainter. Life went on. The sun burned off the morning mists and the city began waking up. For three days, the plane—whose color was a rather beautiful blue-gray—had been looking for a cloudless city. Now it had found one. This information was immediately transmitted, and the plane returned to base with all possible speed.

An hour later, a second plane flew over Hiroshima, this one a bomber. It flew at a very high altitude, so that you could hear but not see it, hard as people tried. The local military command was surprised. Normally planes flew in squadron groups. For a few tense moments they held their breath, waiting for the bombs to hit, or for the sound of more planes arriving. But nothing happened. Maybe, they thought, the pilot had flown off course. Maybe his radio had malfunctioned, and that first plane had been sent out to search for it. The authorities decided not to sound the air-raid sirens. The sound stopped, as if the plane had suddenly vanished. What had actually happened was it had veered sharply, and the high-altitude winds carried the sound of the propellers in a different direction. The B-29 had changed course because its mission was completed: It had dropped one four-ton bomb. Small, rigid parachutes deployed to slow its descent. For optimal effect the bomb was to detonate nineteen hundred feet above its target. The moment that followed was surely a strange one for those who watched the slowly descending spot of light, one that humanity had not known for many years. They might have felt what the American Indians experienced when a

Gatling gun was being trained on them, or what animals with no previous contact with humans experience as they face their first hunter. Here was a unique moment in a century of iron and fire, in the silence of a cloudless sky that seemed to have absorbed time and space, with the exception of this tiny brilliant dot heading toward them. Then the moment vaporized. The bomb had gone off at precisely the designated height.

By the time he had reached this point in the letter, Kumo was startled to discover that it was nearly dark. His right hand was cramping. He ended the letter by telling Virginie that a second would follow, finishing the story; he would write it tomorrow. At long last he would speak openly of what had happened to him. The next day he waited for Virginie to call. All morning he sat at the desk in the library, trying to write the second letter. Nothing came to him, and he gave up. He went back to the library in the evening. He opened the glass doors, went out onto the small balcony overlooking Rue Lamarck, and he jumped.

As she returned to her hotel room Sunday evening around half past seven, Virginie was wondering why things always got sadder. As she passed the front desk she was handed a red-and-blue envelope but didn't open it. She contacted an overnight shipping company, wrapped *The Abercrombie Protocol* as carefully as she could, and wrote the Rue Lamarck address on the package. She went down to the front desk to wait for the messenger, who arrived in twenty minutes because she had been willing to pay the premium for immediate shipment. She wondered what Kumo was doing at that moment.

———

Leaping into space is no easy thing. Kumo knew this because at the last moment his foot got stuck, and he was thrown head-forward. Then his shoulder struck the balcony on the floor below, slowing his fall. Twenty-five feet further down his body bounced off the metal roof of a delivery truck, rolled down the windshield, and finally landed on the street. His spinal column was broken in two places. He had thought that perhaps when his brain hit the pavement it might make a pretty cloud; this didn't happen. Kumo lost consciousness but he was still alive when they put him in the ambulance. He didn't die that evening, or at the moment Virginie was wondering what he was doing. Nor did he die the next day, or in the days that followed.

Virginie went back up to her room and opened the envelope. She smiled when she saw that it contained a letter from Kumo. She was reading it when someone from his staff remembered to call and relay the news. She threw her things into her suitcase and jumped into a cab to Waterloo Station. It was Sunday; the last train had left, and there wouldn't be another until the following day.

Sitting in his living room, Richard Abercrombie was feeling pleased with himself. He had never known quite what to do with that bloody book. He had always thought he might donate it, except what institution would want to house such an oddity once they knew what it actually contained? Before he had given it to Virginie he told her what he knew about its provenance, and about his grandfather and namesake.

In 1889, to commemorate the 100th anniversary of the French Revolution, Paris decided to host a World Fair. What had happened in France a century earlier had made the crowned heads of Europe tremble on their thrones. Paris was the capital of the civilized world. During the course of the nineteenth century the center shifted. France was gradually being turned into a backwater—as handsome as an old medallion and as faded as an antique jewel. In 1889 there was little wattage left over from the Age of Enlightenment and Paris was now essentially a dying star. However, to commemorate the Revolution, the City of Light would summon up its strengths for one last great effort and do something in really grand style, even though it had already become what it would remain: a theme park for paunchy amusement-seekers from the industrialized world. They came by the thousands, porting their own postcard-makers and cameras with which they took pictures of the city from every point of view and in every *quartier, quartiers* that soon were no longer worth looking at because they had become so overexposed by these silly fools, to the point that one wondered whether any part of the city was really worth looking at anymore, any neighborhood whose beauty had not been lost.

In 1889, at least, Parisians still believed in the existence of Paris, and the French still believed in one France, indivisible. So the organizers of the *Exposition Universelle,* as it was called, worked frantically long days. They busied themselves with all forms of locomotion, and expounded on the wonders of vaccination. They issued invitations and organized subcommittees. Inspired by the Progress of Civilization and its offshoots, the organizers deemed themselves progressives, celebrating the idea that the shadows formed by religious superstition continued to recede everywhere throughout the world, and that soon there would be no more priests and no more reason to wage war. The luckiest of these dreamers would die before the summer of 1914. Meanwhile, Parisian shopkeepers, restaurateurs, and café owners were rubbing their hands in greedy anticipation of the enormous profits they stood to gain. Purveyors of luxury items (careful to eschew politics) prepared their inventories. A few steps away from the House of Chanel on Rue Cambon, Alice Cadolle invented the bra. Soon the garter belt (which, said certain waggish wits, had been inspired by the lower level of Gustave Eiffel's tower) would replace the corset. Should they so desire, any woman could dress *in less than an hour* and without assistance from her maid. Beneath the temporary steel-bolted tower set up on the Champs-de-Mars—against which idle writers and other discontents would petition—had been placed the Fountain of Progress. The fountain was a masterpiece of industrial art that continuously recycled its foamy water, thanks to a motor ingeniously hidden under the pool. People admired the technical prowess of the thing and gazed at it silently while their guides explained what it signified— and warned that the water wasn't drinkable.

In 1889 France saw itself as an empire but it was actually a bazaar. Jules Ferry had instituted mandatory instruction. He had also devastated the lives of peasants working the rice fields far from Paris, peasants so different from France's own that no one could confuse the two. There were hordes of American tourists in Paris. This was the first time they had come over in such numbers and without being drawn by the dream of becoming artists, or indeed without any cultural interests whatever. They traversed the Louvre's gardens en masse without really seeing them, though the gardens had been beautifully prepared and everything sparkled under the bright sun like slightly silly-looking antique toys. No need for the Americans to feel homesick. One of the *Exposition Universelle*'s main attractions during the month of May was Buffalo Bill's Wild West Show. The Fair sought to be truly universal, embracing all nations and races: One exhibit proved that the Algerians knew how to grow grapes and produce wine that they would not themselves consume. A little further on, in the shadow of the Eiffel Tower, some Negroes were placed in a pen. Crowds of people gathered around at quarter past each hour, when the Negroes would emerge from their torpor to pound some grain or sing a song; the more energetic among them performed a dance. Ladies with parasols recoiled when these fierce-looking men bared their teeth. An entire Cairo street had been reconstituted in the Seventh Arrondissement. The city's most popular bordellos, having anticipated the demand for variety, had brought in Hottentots and Kanaks; Annamites were all the rage, far more popular that year than Jewesses. For the occasion, representatives of Van Houten, chocolate merchants and coffee makers, were offering free tours of an Indonesian village reconstituted entirely from original building materials.

Finally, in every university lecture hall, in every conference room in every ministry building, and sometimes even in tents and dark backrooms, congresses were convened. The Congress of the Rationalist Union, for example, and the Congress of European Steelworkers. There were congresses of mushroom growers and numismatists, of organic chemists; there was the Congress of the Theosophical Society. It was therefore only fitting and natural that the director of the observatory in Montsouris Park—with the approval of the president of every learned society—convene, in September of 1889, the World Meteorological Congress.

While all these gatherings of scholars and scientists were taking place, the clouds floated by, indifferent as ever to human activities. And for their part, the organizers and visitors paid no heed of them. When they glanced upward it was only to decide whether to have their aperitif outside on the terrace or in the Egyptian Café or the Brazil Pavilion. We were in the modern age now. No one was interested in clouds unless they were threatening. On the morning of September 20, 1889, around 9 A.M., Paris seemed to be suddenly enveloped by a dark penumbra moving from west to east. It started to rain. Out came the umbrellas. Everyone cursed the weather. Nearly everyone, actually, for this was the first day of the World Meteorological Congress. The French

Meteorological Society had planned everything beautifully: The meeting would take place in a vast amphitheater in the hospital at Salpêtrière, which boasted a brand-new glass ceiling that had been specially designed by the hospital's administrators. The rain started to pound softly against the glass at 9:25, just at the moment when the Minister of Agriculture had proclaimed the opening of the congress. The rain was welcomed as a friend, almost as a participant in the proceedings. Among the gathered, those who had predicted rain modestly accepted the compliments of their colleagues; some among them thought, with that delicious frisson that comes of heresy, that they didn't really like rain, but were careful not to reveal this to anyone.

It rained hard, the water pelting against the glass. Meteorology was a new science. Indeed the congress was intended to measure the extent of what was not known, and to offer grandiose opinions about what kind of research ought to be undertaken. One speaker followed another, each offering his hypothesis regarding such things as the formation of cyclones, or the dissipation of fog at sea, or how the calculation of air humidity might be refined; they spoke well and in strong voices and were heartily applauded for their efforts. And yet not one meteorologist—not a single one among them—could offer an explanation for the rain that was beating down right over their heads. Worse, not one of them even guessed at the complexities that lay behind the phenomenon. The subject of rain was both too basic and too comprehensive to have captured their attention. Asked to explain why it was raining, the more sophisticated of the meteorologists gathered there would have offered the following: Moisture in the air had reached a sufficient quantity that water particles had merged and begun the process of condensation; this condensation had formed what we called a cloud; and when the air's humidity reached a saturation point, too heavy to stay in the air, rain fell. That was it, more or less.

Actually, the formation of clouds depends upon a series of overlapping factors—the atmosphere, for example. How much water the ambient air can hold depends upon temperature: At zero degrees Celsius, the air can hold barely five grams of water per cubic meter; at twenty degrees Celsius it can become supersaturated and easily contain seventeen grams of water per cubic meter. Nonetheless a significant amount of water in the air isn't reason enough for a rain cloud to form. Tiny particles have to be present, and they can be of varying origins and natures: marine salt, volcanic ash, the gas produced by cars and planes, a grain of desert sand vaulted high into the air by a fierce wind. These particles ally themselves with tiny electrified particles that roam the terrestrial atmosphere. Their union creates the basis for condensation. Then and only then is rain possible. Nonetheless, even if all these elements align, it still might not rain, because the water drops that make up clouds have little to do with those that fall and which we call "rain."

The water in clouds takes the shape of tiny droplets whose radii range between a thousandth and a hundredth of a millimeter in length; a cubic centimeter of cloud can thus easily contain one thousand, sometimes as many as fifteen hundred, of these spherical droplets. They don't get mixed up together in the center of the cloud. The tiny currents of air that their displacement creates won't permit such coalescences. The droplets remain isolated, powerless. Naturally such tiny objects fall very slowly. Those that break away from the protective cover of the cloud evaporate instantaneously, and across the entire surface of the cloud other droplets form to compensate for that evaporation. To the human eye a cloud seems to move, but what it is in fact doing is engaging in a constant process of evaporation and reformation. Sometimes droplets do aggregate around the tiny hardened particles of condensation. As they aggregate they grow fatter and fatter, heavier and heavier, achieving a diameter that can vary between one and a half and three millimeters. These are the droplets that fall, and as they fall, they join together with other droplets to form drops, which can reach dimensions of up to six millimeters. When these larger drops manage to reach the ground we can say it is raining.

On Monday, September 20, 1889, toward eleven in the morning, complete silence accompanied one of the greatest meteorologists of his day as he surged toward the stage. The rain had stopped. The arrival of William S. Williamsson was much anticipated; it was expected to be the day's highlight. He spoke an English that was correct but coarse, upsetting his refined colleagues, and over the years had forged an appearance that matched his subject: He had the leonine head of a visionary genius, a full beard, and long, wavy hair, as fine as if it had been spun from silver ore. His powerful upper body was planted on legs that were short but looked as sturdy as a mountaineer's; his long arms were muscular. It was difficult to look at Williamsson and not be reminded of some great ape, particularly given the manner in which he swung his way up the steps leading to the stage. He took hold of the podium as if he intended to wrench it from its anchorage. The audience was expectant, and of this he was well aware. He saw himself as the main event and had been dozing with his eyes open through the earlier presentations and speeches.

Among those gathered to listen to him—scholars who had come to the Congress without intending to speak and also without their wives, and who had been busy trying to make eye contact with their female neighbors whom they hoped to bed in the next night or two—was one individual who sat at the far end of a table reserved for the meeting's organizers, and who presented a striking contrast with Williamsson. There was nothing at all memorable about this individual; he was one of those people one might greet in the street, confusing him for someone else. Because he resembled no one in particular, he resembled nearly everyone. Indifferent to those who now pointed him out, and to their female neighbors who politely and perhaps charitably flashed their eyes at him while inclining their heads, Richard Abercrombie waited, impassive. He was a small man with a moustache. His hairline had receded and left him with a pronounced, veined forehead. He seemed unperturbed by anything, and appeared to be listening with rapt attention to Williamsson, who just now was gesturing with aplomb and offering his compliments to the organizers. Abercrombie stared straight ahead, his eyes hidden behind thick brows. His large sideburns contained hints of red. He was the archetype of the English gentleman, both physically and in terms of outlook. He had agreed to sit at this table only after his dear friend and distinguished colleague Williamsson had insisted he do so. He hated Williamsson passionately, categorically, and with the constant and inexhaustible rage that one man of science can feel for another. Williamsson heartily returned the sentiment. There are points of view that will never be reconciled, and these two men had never found common ground on the principle subject of their research—clouds. Naturally, being the world's outstanding experts in this area of meteorological research, fellows as it were of the same chimera, and despite being separated by bodies of water and opposing temperaments, Abercrombie and Williamsson were united by their ambitions. For ten years they had worked together. To the world they seemed like fast friends.

Beginning the previous evening, a persistent rumor had been circulating (meaning the better-informed—and usually more malicious—had informed the less-well-informed about something while at the same time enjoining them to secrecy). It was being rumored that this congress, which should have represented Abercrombie and Williamsson's hour of triumph as a team, would sound the death knell of their friendship. Years of fruitful collaboration had helped them to make critical contributions to understanding the most complex of meteorological issues, such as cloud classification, storm prediction on open water, and the phenomenon of fog. Two years before this meeting, the Scot and the Swede, the first through patient and methodical labors, the latter through grandiloquent rhetorical gestures, had together conceived of, written, and published a new version of Luke Howard's cloud classification. Their new taxonomy had had the good fortune of placating everyone from archconservative reactionaries to passionate progressives. Even more importantly, it had won the general support of the international meteorological community, which unanimously judged it to be a decisive step forward, one that did not in fact replace Howard's basic categories but enriched them. From the very first moment, readers of the Williamsson-Abercrombie classification refinements had been seduced by a stroke of inspiration that is the mark of genius, in science as in all fields of human endeavor. The two men audaciously regrouped clouds into two classes, each composed of five distinct types: On the one side were the cloudlike forms, either individual or bunched together, that are most commonly observed during dry weather; on the other are the more extensive, shroudlike formations that are common during wet weather. Even more cleverly— this had been Abercrombie's inspiration—they had given clouds appealingly picturesque and suggestive names to accompany their Latin versions: The individual clouds were known as "sheep" (*cirrocumulus*) and even "fat sheep" (*altocumulus*); within the *cumulus* formation one found "rain clouds" or "cloud stacks" or "waved clouds"; the stratus became "elevated fog." It was all part of an effort to democratize meteorology and was greeted with enthusiasm, particularly by the amateurs, who for twenty years had far outnumbered professional meteorologists, and who were grateful to Williamsson and Abercrombie for making it all so eminently accessible.

The World Congress of 1889 was the first to take place since the announcement of the new classification, and from the beginning the two men had received warm encomia from their colleagues, smiles from the ladies whose visitor's books they signed, and requests for further clarifications from neophytes. The Howard Classification, Updated and Emended by Abercrombie & Williamsson, was the new authority. The friendly rivalry between its authors had provoked commentary and not a few smiles. When those who tried found nothing scandalous about either man, they embroidered what little they did know, or made something up. Williamsson was the son of farmers from the region of Östergötland and had always managed to win scholarships and fellowships for himself and those who worked with him. But over time he had started to earn a reputation for hoarding lucrative posts. Hence he occupied two chaired professorships at the university, in addition to being the Meteorologist to the King of Sweden, the Special Advisor to the Secretary for Maritime Affairs, and the Head of the Union for Deep-Sea Fishing. Abercrombie was the scion of a wealthy and prestigious family: For centuries his male ancestors had sacrificed their lives—either from rare tropical diseases or on the field of battle—for the greater glory of Scotland and, by extension, the British crown. His grandfather had been killed in a naval engagement against the French in the Mediterranean. As far as clouds were concerned, Abercrombie was an enlightened and gifted amateur. He had joined forces with Williamsson after first engaging him in a lengthy correspondence involving that very complex question of whether fog should actually be considered a low-altitude cloud or an entirely distinct meteorological phenomenon. Their correspondence led to the publication of a first article, cosigned by both parties, entitled, "Notes toward a Systematic Definition of Fogs, Mists, and Drizzle That Form above the Ground."

One particular story involving William S. Williamsson had been in circulation among meteorological societies for a number of years. It began twenty years before, involved Williamsson's scientific start, and was not particularly flattering.

By 1870, European ship owners and maritime operators had fully embraced the idea that weather forecasting was worth gold. Delaying or accelerating the departure of a vessel filled with precious woods, for example, in order to keep it from getting becalmed or to take advantage of prevailing winds, could mean the difference between financial ruin and success. Imagine the money to be made on the stock market if one knew in advance when there would be a frost on Aquitaine's vineyards, or when the rains would arrive in Prussia. What were needed were weathermen who were more than mere dabblers and enlightened amateurs but true scientists. As a young man, Williamsson had sensed this sea change and welcomed it, for he knew that it might mean long-term and substantial financial and social benefits for him and others like him, indeed improving the lot of all those who

lived in servitude to the land and to the whims of the sky.
Williamsson would liberate them forever from the tyranny
of muddy fields. That was the tacit mission his parents had
chosen for the youngest and most gifted of their children,
and he had obeyed their wishes. Indeed, rather than chafing
under this yoke of responsibility, the boy went at it with
prodigal vivacity. By the age of twenty he had become the
personal assistant to the great Swedish meteorologist Jürgen
Svensson, a man whom Williamsson had so admired starting
at the age of ten that he had taken "Svensson" as his middle
name.

Beginning when he was a sixty-five-year-old, Svensson,
the director of the Royal Meteorological Institute in Uppsala,
was increasingly being turned to by ship captains, owners, and
merchants seeking reliable predictions about weather patterns. A child of the Age of Rousseau, a man who decried the
excessive mechanization that was beginning to dominate
meteorological observation, Svensson began ceding to their
wishes and offering predictions, though he rejected the whole
notion of weather forecasting, the way a serious chemist
would be appalled if asked to concoct potions to cure bald-
ness or alleviate gastric distress. Svensson kept with him always a note he had received from an elderly Luke Howard,
encouraging the young Swede and fellow cloud admirer in
his research. Svensson preferred watercolor sketches of the
weather to abstract lines symbolizing climatic fronts. Nonetheless he did not refuse to see the ship owners, insurance
agents, and others who came seeking his advice about maritime routes or anxious to get his thoughts regarding weather
patterns over water. These men paid good money, money

that funded his most basic research. He remained an aristocrat, however, and never really understood why such knowledge wasn't satisfactory for its own sake.

Such was the charming, quaint man Williamsson had
chosen as his mentor. He served Svensson with filial devotion for nearly twenty years. Finally he decided that he had
learned all that he could from the old man. Soon to turn
seventy-three, Svensson didn't seem any less active than he
ever had been, and exhibited no interest whatever in retiring.
The winter of 1879 was unseasonably cold and seemingly
endless. The weekly bulletins issued by the Royal Institute
in Uppsala at the end of winter were objects of keen attention throughout Sweden. The fishing boat operators and
passenger ship managers were eager to go into full operation.
Everyone in Sweden turned their eyes to Svensson. Svensson
hesitated before giving the green light; he saw no end to winter. As so often happens in these cases, resentful about the
loss of income, the merchants ended up blaming the messenger. Certain newspapers began publishing disparaging remarks
about the institute, the cost of maintaining it, its outmoded
ways, and the arrogance of its director. Svensson showed these
articles with great sadness to his young disciple, who sympa-
thized with his mentor.

On Monday, March 16, 1879, the weather in Sweden
turned mild, almost springlike. The most recent bulletin of
the Royal Institute, published the previous Friday, announced
increasing cold and violent storms. A powerful union of the
fishing industry had canceled a trawling expedition based on
the announcement. Passenger lines declared they had had

enough, demanding to be allowed to open the lanes to Europe. The thaw continued through Tuesday. The newspapers turned their attention to the Institute. A journalist from the largest newspaper announced a stunning piece of news involving weather prediction. According to one source the Royal Institute should be criticized for not keeping pace with the latest scientific, schematic, and technical advances available to it. Svensson knew that the source had to have come from inside the Institute, and turned for help to Williamsson, who promised to launch an immediate investigation. Happily the warming trend ended on Wednesday and Thursday. Matters quieted down. But everyone waited with feverish anticipation for the bulletin that was to be issued on Friday, March 23. Svensson asked his young disciple whether it wasn't time to use the new methods the journalist had pointed out. Williamsson had no difficulty convincing Svensson that such a move would encourage the most rabid of their detractors. On Thursday night, Svensson, as was his habit, prepared his bulletin using data given to him by Williamsson. He noted with some relief that the data suggested that beautiful dry weather would settle over Sweden for the entirety of the following week, along with seasonal temperatures. Svensson's bulletin went without delay to ship owners, chambers of commerce, and passenger lines.

Williamsson was questioned by the investigating committee looking into the catastrophic bulletin of March 23. He denied giving Professor Svensson imprecise information, saying that he wished that this were the case, that he might have spared his venerable mentor the shame of what resulted from his mistakes. Here we enter the realm of speculation.

The more charitable of Williamsson's detractors accused him of giving Svensson flawed data; the less charitable were convinced that Williamsson, sensing that his chance had come, had not only been that inside informant but had deliberately given Svensson flawed information; that he had known perfectly well that spring would not come to Sweden for another week; and that the young Williamsson had not wanted to expose himself to hostility from the powerful merchants. Because of the bulletin issued on Friday, March 23, dozens of vessels went to sea at dawn the next morning. Commercial links between Frisia and Sweden were reestablished, and passenger boats went into full operation. On Saturday the weather stayed calm. However, between Sunday and Tuesday, thirteen hundred Swedes lost their lives, as did five hundred more from other countries. The first storm swept the entire country from north to south within a matter of hours on Sunday afternoon; a second and more violent storm struck on Monday night and lasted through Thursday; it followed almost exactly the same path. This was the one that swept over the fishing vessels just before they returned to their ports. Svensson didn't die for three days. The bullet that he had fired into his mouth came out his ear; he had chosen the wrong caliber. He lived long enough to name Williamsson his heir and successor.

During Svensson's funeral when Williamsson spoke of his years of apprenticeship to the great man his eyes brimmed with tears. He emphasized the importance of continuing the great man's work, and that though it was yet too early to draw conclusions or to cast blame, one could say that the whole program of modernization being undertaken at the Royal

Institute stemmed from the lives lost due to that tragic mis-take. William Svensson Williamsson outlined his views with great energy and conviction. In July 1879 he was named di-rector of the Royal Meteorological Institute.

Thus the story that accompanied the man speaking just now at the meeting in Paris. No one would ever have dared to ask him about it. He was powerful, and he forgot nothing.

$\mathcal{N}ow$, *ten years* after taking Svensson's place, Williamsson was speaking before a congress of his peers. In his oration he evoked the great city of Paris, where they were all gathered, and its role as the world's capital; he touched upon the magic of electric storms; he expounded upon the leading lights of nephology—the term he was proposing for this new science of cloud analysis—and how necessary it was to spread the gospel of this science to the ends of the known world; and he urged his listeners to consider how critical it was to universalize Howard's classification (as emended in 1887). This, he said, was how the clouds would finally reveal to us their deepest secrets.

The hall erupted in applause. Rather than stop there, Williamsson paused for a moment, and then launched into a vision of the future. What would the year 2000 be like from a *nephological* perspective? It was presumptuous to think in these terms, naturally, and yet—and yet—one might reasonably make a few predictions without being guilty of an excess of optimism. Deserts would be things of the past. By then we will have learned to move clouds and to control the rains. No sand anywhere. Or perhaps we might have saved one desert for posterity, the Sahara probably, smallish in dimensions now and useful mainly for balloon excursions and for camel rides. You could hunt gazelles and fox and when evening came to the sheltered part of a wadi where you had set up camp, you could ask the local authorities through some means of radio-electric communication for a light cloud cover, to heat up the air and permit those ladies who so desire to sleep outside in a refreshing atmosphere. And that wouldn't be all, because they who control the clouds also control agriculture. Chronic famine would be a thing of the past among all the savages of all races; tomato fields would cover the Sahel and waving oceans of wheat would flood the plains of the Kalahari. No longer would thousands of farmers in India or the Far East live in fear the monsoon season would come late, or that rainfall would be too plentiful or too sparse. Wherever necessary, rice could be grown all year round. Rain would fall upon the ancient Negev Desert; and the manna that God had given his Chosen People would become available for Modern Man to offer his brother. London's inhabitants would no longer need to heat their homes six months of the year, and the air over that magnificent city would regain its original purity. Only the elegant city of Paris, already blessed with clement weather, would not require modification.

As they listened, soothed by the warm and powerful tones of Williamsson, the women half closed their eyes and had visions of perpetual spring in Madrid, in Sydney, in Haiti, and wondered what the fashions would be; the men forgot their grumbling stomachs, so flattered did they feel about this exaltation of their meteorological prowess. Williamsson himself was lifted by his own élan, and for about ten minutes had periodically been resting his gaze upon a buxom, dark-haired widow sitting, all aquiver, in the sixth row. Finally, well aware when enough was enough, Williamsson began his per-oration. In the year 2000, continuing on a track that began here, we will have understood where clouds derive their energy. We will have domesticated their ascending powers: Our "aeronefs" will silently and gracefully glide from one continent to another, far above all of nature's marvels. There will no longer be a distinction between the fertile regions of the world and the infertile regions; the earth will be a vast garden in which we will live in the Golden Age about which the mythologies and religions have informed us; man will be good; our grandchildren will see the desolate plains of Canaan blossom again. The science of our descendants will fulfill the prophecies of our ancestors.

He knew it was time to wind things up. Someone in the audience had coughed; more coughing would soon follow. Others were shifting in their seats to cover up the gurgling of their stomachs. Only the widow in the sixth row, vibrating like a gelatinous terrine, was hanging upon his lips, his beard, his powerful torso. Williamsson would not sleep alone that night, and that thought very nearly distracted him from the critical matter now at hand. While pretending to rearrange his papers, he looked over the audience, which was on its feet and applauding thunderously (both because of the way in which he had moved them and because he'd been sensible enough to quit early). He realized that he had to seize the moment while it was still his to seize, while the applause had passed its apex but still going strong. Williamsson smote his sheaf of papers against the podium and, Caesar-like, raised his arm. The room went silent immediately. His assistants circulated and positioned themselves at the end of each row. Subdued, the audience members sat down. To anyone wearing an official ribbon of the congress, the assistants handed an object, which smelled of fresh glue. It was a booklet, nearly square-shaped, roughly thirty centimeters on a side. The title was printed in gray letters across the front, in German, French, English, and Swedish. Its arrival was greeted with murmurs of approval. Williamsson had finally completed the first *International Cloud Atlas.* The great man at the podium permitted his colleagues to take stock of what it was they held in their hands. It was not a thick tome, but it contained unrivaled riches. Inside were ten colored lithographs, each corresponding to a type of cloud from the Howard Classification (Updated and Emended by Abercrombie & Williamsson). Each was followed by an explanatory text, informing the reader that these works had been executed by artists to specifications provided by scientific experts and without hesitation, even when it became a question of sacrificing Art at the altar of Science. Each lithograph was, in short, a representation of the Truth.

Standing at the podium, Williamsson modestly lowered his eyes, and thanked everyone who had worked with him on the project. How he would have liked to name them individually but there were simply too many. Finally he had come to the core of the matter: However imperfect, these images would allow his valued colleagues to help usher Nephology into a new era—the Era of Science. None of the forms depicted in these works can be found in nature (this was greeted by a disapproving murmur from the audience), but that was precisely why they were so useful (greeted first by silence, then scattered murmurs of approval). One must not ask of a cloud atlas that it be beautiful from an artistic point of view, for that would distract the reader from Truth; so, too, those landscapes depicted by artists, even obscure artists, find their greatest justification in the degree to which they provide a context for the examination of the sky. And it will not be said at the moment of this centenary of the French Revolution that the World Meteorological Society would side with reactionaries! Tomorrow we will commission other chromolithographs, if the means can be found; the finest watercolorists shall be put into the service by the finest scientists and thus Art will reside again in the bosom of Science, which it never left to begin with, and under its leadership give birth to the first *International Cloud Atlas* worthy of the name. Our descendants in the century to come, inhabiting a world at peace, will speak with pride about this congress. *They dared,* they will say, *and they were right to dare.*

There was to be a follow-up session, but the audience, nearly regressing to the enthusiasm of their student days, thumped the bottom of their chairs in unison, hailing the new master of world meteorology. The president brought the meeting to a close; the follow-up session would be postponed until the afternoon, he announced. The audience filed out and headed into the cafés along the Boulevard de l'Hôpital. At the foot of the dome of Salpêtrière, Williamsson was surrounded by admirers, congratulating him and inviting him to breakfast, lunch, or dinner. He declined all offers. He needed to return to his hotel near the Opéra to rest a little and prepare for the next day's meeting. Such discipline was greeted with appreciative whispers. Just as he turned to stride up the boulevard, the large lady with dark hair appeared, offering to share her cab; she happened to be going in the same direction. They left together, Williamsson acknowledging his admirers from the window. By the time the hansom reached Place de la Bastille Williamsson's benefactress was on her back with her dress hiked up, biting on the carriage curtain so that her ecstatic grunts were not overheard by the driver.

No one was disappointed by the cancellation of the question-and-answer session, no one except one man, forgotten in all the commotion. This, of course, was Richard Abercrombie. He showed not the least emotion when handed a copy of the *International Cloud Atlas*. He didn't rise up and denounce Williamsson, who hadn't even told him about this publication. The Swede had asked him as a favor not to speak about the atlas at the Paris Congress, using as a pretext their growing differences in opinion. Abercrombie had agreed. By a happy coincidence he was to be the first speaker of the afternoon.

That afternoon, when Abercrombie was preparing to give his speech, there were a number of empty seats in the amphitheater, though the president of the session had postponed the start until three. Professor Williamsson sent his regrets that he might not be able to attend, having suddenly felt indisposed. At that moment he was lying on his back with his hands grasping the buttocks of the large lady, who was astride him, her breasts smacking moistly against her stomach. The more elderly participants of the congress had seized upon the arrival of the cloud atlas as an excuse, and were vigorously toasting it in several of the city's palaces of pleasure. After all, what else were these damnable congresses good for? This portion of the audience was no longer able to stiffen sufficiently for sex but, today at least, that fact didn't sadden them particularly; they were drunk. When finally Abercrombie took the podium at 3:30 he was not surprised to learn that he had been bested. He remembered now that Williamsson had asked whether he would be willing to switch the order of their presentations. The thought nearly made him smile. During the extended lunch break he had decided to go against tradition at these congresses and simply talk of what he most cared about. He put his prepared remarks back in his briefcase—the paper, rather technical in nature, had been entitled "Climatic Observation Methodology on Open Seas." He was going to do what he had never done before—extemporize. Through the windows at the rear of the amphitheater he could see lines of cloud rushing to the east.

Abercrombie did little public speaking and wasn't particularly good at it. He wasn't witty and said only what was necessary. No one was listening to him, so preoccupied were they by the process of digestion. He told himself that something might come of this. Like someone shooting an arrow, he would send his idea into the air not knowing where it would land, or if someday someone would find it and be interested enough to take it home. Just as the surface of the planet revealed an impressive variety of human diversity, intoned Abercrombie, so, too, for species of clouds, which would naturally vary by latitude. The artistic license of the chromolithography in the Atlas permitted one to question its reliability. Helio-typography, as it was once called, or, if one preferred, helio-engraving, as was used more recently, or, as it was now being called, photography, offered the only means of looking at something with the requisite objectivity and without prejudice.

Abercrombie was boring his audience. A small commotion announced Williamsson's late arrival. He gestured grandly to his colleague on the stage, while wondering whether he was still reeking of perfume and sex and whether those nearest him might notice. To them he seemed to be considering some serious matter; in actuality he was trying to dislodge with his tongue a hair that had gotten stuck between his teeth. Abercrombie had to interrupt his talk to return the salute but managed not to lose his train of thought. He would, he said, take advantage of the presence of his most eminent colleague to offer a word about Williamsson's vision of the world in which clouds might be harnessed by man. He begged permission to temper his own enthusiasm for such a vision, because even if we learned how a cloud is born, lives, and dies, we will never know how the man-made version will behave. What we need to do first is to photograph clouds throughout the world *that we might see.* Whoever was fit to undertake such a task would have to be a resolute man of science, and moreover familiar with daguerreotypes. This individual would travel the entire globe and bring back images of clouds at all the latitudes, so that the whole debate might be reabsorbed. Moreover, he, Richard Abercrombie, volunteered to undertake this himself. He would leave the very next month and asked if his estimable colleague William Svensson Williamsson might be willing to accompany him, so that upon their return they might together publish a true "universal cloud atlas."

Abercrombie's remarks were greeted with restrained applause. Williamsson rose to his feet and strode toward him, his arms spread open. He climbed the stage and warmly embraced his adversary. He regretted that he would have to refuse the invitation made by his honored colleague, as he was prevented from leaving because of a number of duties. Moreover, he was but a humble working man, while Abercrombie had the ability to place his personal fortune at the service of science. He should depart immediately on this mission, and go with the knowledge that he, Williamsson, would be thinking of him at every step of the way, hoping to be kept informed about its progress. Let an official proclamation be issued by this congress, formally appointing Richard Abercrombie to lead this grand enterprise, one worthy of the country just now extending its hospitality. The congress's participants raised their hands to second the nomination of this new cloud commissioner. During the course of the afternoon two young scientists offered their first presentations at the podium. Abercrombie returned to his hotel on the Boulevard Saint-Marcel on foot. Two days later he was in London, where he realized that he had not so much as once visited Paris while he was there. As for Williamsson, he put the whole ridiculous episode out of his mind; the important thing was to be rid of this exasperatingly upright and starchy Scot.

Several hours later, his head clearing a little, Akira Kumo noted that he was not yet dead. He was in a hospital, and feeling no pain, and not dead. He would have preferred to have avoided precisely this turn of events and had been aware that jumping out a window was not the surest route to mortality. Like everyone else he had heard those miraculous stories of survival—about suicides being carried by the wind, or unlucky enough to have landed in a thick garden hedge, or on a garbage pile they had not known would be there. He had jumped without premeditation. Now he would be fussed over by nurses, become the focus of patronizing pity from the head doctor, and be subjected to insinuating questions by a psychologist, a psychiatric intern, even the clinic's chaplain. Worse, he would have to start over living again, to repair his battered body; it would be several days, perhaps several weeks, before he would be able to try again.

He drifted back to the moment when he was still lying on Rue Lamarck, regaining consciousness, looking up at the sky and all the rest of it. Later he would think about the distress his actions would cause his staff.

He had watched the delicate *cirrus* clouds about six miles over the roofs of Paris, clouds so light and airy that they seemed made of the finest muslin, like scratches left by some unknown animal. He had often thought these clouds transformed the sky into a sort of beach where the tide had deposited them. He knew *cirrus* well, and was proud of knowing that, in this latitude at least, they generally indicated the arrival of bad weather. *Cirrus* were his favorites. He took them for oracles, mysterious signs, though aware that he would never be able to decipher them in any definitive fashion. When he saw them he sometimes thought of sperm trickling down a rose-colored vagina, or sperm floating on the surface of bathwater.

But this time the cirrus clouds didn't symbolize anything. They were simply there, above him. He would never succeed in interpreting them. Nonetheless, that wouldn't diminish their ineffable and discreet beauty. For perhaps the first time, Kumo loved them for what they actually were. Then he lost consciousness; the initial shock had worn off and his shattered left leg was beginning to put him in agonies of pain.

Deprived of their one attentive observer, the clouds continued to float over Rue Lamarck, existing for nothing and for no one. The vast majority of Parisians paid no attention to the *cirrus* hovering nearly immobile above the stratus zone. From their perch at the upper limit of the terrestrial atmosphere, they were made of ice rather than water. Far below them, their heads down, Parisians walked from one place to another, one nothingness to another, unaware of the clouds' existence, clueless as to how rich and free life beneath the impassive sky might possibly be.

Several passersby on the street pretended not to notice the frail and unmoving body of an old man lying on the pavement. Finally a young man stopped and made a call. Soon enough the people who do the things no one else wants to do arrived; they carefully lifted Kumo into an ambulance. Only twenty-four hours after his leap into the void, Kumo found himself back where he had started. His leg was so destroyed by the fall that the doctors determined it would be impossible to put it in a cast. He was strapped to the bed to prevent any sudden movement during sleep that might permanently damage his spinal column. He had no feeling in his legs. He spent the day on painkillers, slumbering without sleeping. His staff proposed that they put him in his library, his favorite room, except that if he was lying on his back in his library he would have only a limited view of the sky. Kumo told them he didn't care. He was finished with the sky and with clouds. He wanted to be in his bedroom and asked that they close the shutters, a request that was met with some relief, for they were a little concerned that he might regain feeling in his legs and take advantage of this to jump again, headfirst this time.

That Monday, around 8 P.M., Kumo awoke in a better frame of mind. His personal correspondence was brought in, and the first thing he saw was a package from London. He asked where Mademoiselle Latour might be. Shortly thereafter, Virginie arrived at Rue Lamarck.

Kumo smiled when he saw her smile. They didn't talk about his suicide attempt, or about his letter. They didn't talk about anything at all. So content were they to be together that for quite a while they didn't even make eye contact. Finally Virginie spoke a little about Richard Abercrombie, and the service on the hill. Then she unwrapped the package she'd sent from London and presented it to Kumo. Only the first two pages of *The Abercrombie Protocol* contained photographic images of the skies, meticulously referenced in a tiny, impeccable hand. A brief look was enough for Kumo to understand their purpose: For each of the first two categories of the Howard Cloud Classification (As Updated and Emended by Abercrombie & Williamsson) it offered six images. He and Virginie began to discuss them.

Each of the images had been taken in a different place, as the notations indicated. Abercrombie had started with the *cirrocumulus*—in Lisbon, Malta, Cairo, Aden, Madras, Sydney. Each class of cloud featured its own carefully framed and representative collection. The lesson they taught the viewer had a nearly blinding clarity: The heterogeneity of the cloudy forms was inescapable. Abercrombie had proven beyond doubt at the end of the nineteenth century what is obvious to any traveler today: that any simplistic classification would never accommodate the variety of cloud phenomena in the world. And yet, seeing these images on the same page also made it clear to the observer that, different as they were, all these clouds nonetheless merited being called *"cirrocumulus."* The second page, which was devoted to *cumulus* clouds, offered the same conclusion. Was it possible that was why

Abercrombie had stopped collecting images? Whatever the case, the pages that followed (all labeled) were blank, containing neither photographs nor the little adhesive corners to frame them. The classification that he had played a part in establishing remained perfectly operational, perhaps because of its very indeterminacy. But Abercrombie's odd behavior remained a mystery. A man of such moral fiber, universally known for a rectitude bordering on the puritanical, would not cease from pursuing the subject of his research simply because it proved his theories incorrect. One could easily picture such a man presenting his results at the following meteorological congress, which was to take place in Vienna in 1893, ascending to the podium with his images and announcing to the assembly that he had been entirely mistaken in his suppositions. Instead, Abercrombie broke with the scientific community altogether. He kept his *Protocol* to himself, to the end of his life. Kumo quickly turned the pages. Facing one of the blank pages, Abercrombie had started to keep a jumbled sort of journal, consisting of text written in a tiny hand, some sketches, and a number of odd-sounding sayings and maxims. Most disturbing of all were those photographs of women's sexual organs—numbering in the hundreds—on the book's facing pages.

Each of those facing pages contained only four images, much reduced in scale. Their nature had been sufficient to make Abigail, grown more conventional and moderate in her behavior, reluctant to make the book public. The images could not be explained away as having ethnographic or anthropological value. The women posing in them were wearing no clothes; no folk art, jewels, or tattoos were visible. The photographs weren't fuzzy or gauzy in that suggestive style that had been considered charming in photographs of the period. Nor were they as crude as typical pornography. The images were simple, unadorned. Great care had been taken to highlight every detail; in some cases, where it was too plentiful, the woman's pubic hair had been combed apart, or was gently parted by the subject herself. On one line beneath each photograph was a name, presumably that of the woman posing, as well as the location and country where the image had been taken; on the line below that was the date. So, for example, on the upper right-hand corner of page thirty was an image and beneath it was written "Fatya, Tenarive, Island of Madagascar," and beneath that, "6 December 1889." Her abundant hair is jet-black and lustrous; she is photographed from below, offering a clear shot of her labia, which are almost translucent, the flesh between them of a much lighter color, giving off a brilliant, almost nacreous luster. The recto page was covered with drawings, the same design, repeated over and over. Kumo could see they were of shells, animal heads, women's vaginas; a few clouds as well. Each entry was dated.

It was nearly eleven in the evening, and the night nurse came in to prepare Kumo for sleep. During the next few days, Kumo said to Virginie, he would have to be hospitalized. He wondered whether she would be willing to do a full biblio-graphical description of the *Protocol* while he was gone.

Two weeks passed. Virginie returned to find Kumo in his library, strapped to an immobilizing wheelchair. She drew her chair next to him and began to tell the story. To understand Richard Abercrombie and his collection of photographs, she told Kumo in a firm voice that betrayed a hint of pride, one had to begin in the port town of Dartmouth, England, in November 1889. Kumo closed his eyes.

Like any number of creative and somewhat crazy people, Abercrombie believed in order, in doing things precisely and meticulously. Traveling the world to toil away on something as obsessively lunatic as this Universal Atlas would require unwavering personal discipline and the strictest possible application of methodology. He was, as he knew, perfect for the job. Naturally he had established his itinerary before he left and with great care; the organizing principle wasn't efficiency (he wasn't intending to break any speed records) but based on seasons—so that he wouldn't miss any of the striking meteorological phenomena he wished to observe, such as the sunsets of the Australian summer or the monsoons in India. He took three cameras with him, each one alike, simple and sturdy. They were square and capable of taking two images. He took very few developing chemicals, for you could find them nearly anywhere in the world, but he did pack a large supply of paper, to ensure that the images would be homogeneous. To test the cameras he took views of the port at Dartmouth from the boat while waiting to depart and developed them in his cabin. The results were small squares, nine centimeters in length and eight in height. He placed them in the celluloid corners he had already glued into place on the first page of a large album, which had a thick cover composed of tightly woven, bottle-green fabric. He had estimated that in every location he visited he would take approximately sixty images, six each of the ten categories of clouds in the classification system upon which he and Williamsson had collaborated: three day shots, two sets of them, and three at night, again two sets, if at all possible. After he was finished, Abercrombie was determined to return to the exact spot from which he had started, unchanged, bearing immutable truths. He would attend the congress in Vienna in 1893, and his colleagues, feeling guilty that they had ever doubted him, would elect him president of the World Meteorological Society. Then would his life be complete. He would retire to his farm in the Ochill Hills in Scotland, and hunt for hares with his loyal terrier. Eager but shy young scientists would come from the world over seeking his counsel, insisting on calling him "master," despite his protestations. A delegation would come for a visit on the grand event of his seventieth birthday. He would die following a lengthy illness, bathed in the tearful affection of his faithful servants. They would make a death mask, and place his brain in a jar of formaldehyde, to preserve it for posterity. His terrier would be inconsolable; the cemetery keeper would find the poor animal lying dead on the freshly dug grave of his master, his little heart having given out.

When Abercrombie left the port at Dartmouth on November 28, 1889, a few minutes after midnight, he was forty-seven years old and still a virgin. For a number of years, as he noted in his journal, he had even abstained from masturbation. Achieving the full potential of his genius required chastity. When he returned to England, he was no longer a virgin. Many other things about him had changed as well. But in November of 1889 he was setting out on yet another scientific voyage, a little longer and more exotic than others, perhaps, but otherwise not at all different. He had already been to Canada and Iceland and Spain. He had come back better informed, nothing more.

Abercrombie was a man of his time; he traveled with a bible and three hundred pounds of luggage. He waxed his moustache every day, his long sideburns were neatly trimmed. His boots, which had elaborate lacing, were always polished, and his hatwear was impeccably maintained. His watch and fob shone, the collars of his monogrammed shirts heavily starched. He was a member of the Royal Meteorological Society, the Academy of Sciences, and an honorary member of the Meteorological Society of the Southern Territories. He was the author of two works that were universally admired: *Principles of Meteorological Prediction/Forecasting,* with its 63 pages of text and its 65 illustrations, including six color plates; and a book called simply *The Weather* (472 pages, 96 illustrations), which had become since publication one of the standard references on the subject. Abercrombie possessed the kind of personal courage that impresses the simpleminded and astounds foreigners: One day, in the smoking room of the Meteorological Society of Edinburgh, while debating a member who believed that human fate was absolutely predetermined and that human will would never amount to anything, Abercrombie accidentally severed the tip of his pinkie with a cigar cutter. While applying a tourniquet, made from his own handkerchief, he had countered, to the amazement of his opponent, with a brilliant refutation that had carried the day. Men such as Abercrombie do not change. Like the stalwart vessels of Her Royal Majesty's Navy, they impassively traverse the world's waters—cutting as the blade of a knife, precise as a chronometer. When they died there were always others to take their place.

His intention was to return from this voyage with a book; what was curious was that he already knew what that book would be. As his ship steamed out of Dartmouth's port harbor he worked on the title in his head, then spoke it out loud to the skies: *The Seas and Skies of Various Latitudes.* It would have as a subtitle, one of which he was already quite proud—*In Search of Weather.* It would be an extraordinary book. He knew this; he could feel it. For three centuries countless explorers, adventurers, and scientists had published accounts of their voyages, and for three centuries booksellers had sold them by the yard. Each one pretended to originality, but actually they all told the same stories about how the author had been forced to eat insects or reptiles or had comical or tragic misadventures with natives whom they'd had to pacify with either gifts or guns. Abercrombie had read enough of these travelogues to realize that their authors, whether innocently or not, shamelessly plagiarized their predecessors. He also knew that by 1889 everything had been done, described, analyzed, and dissected. The world had been covered, and for all time. On the shelves of the British Library the attentive reader could find books about every manner of man or beast or vegetation, tomes about every mountain and rock, every shell and fossil. He knew this to be so because he himself had fed upon them and in the process formed that strange exoskeleton that we call "culture."

Nonetheless, he believed that his book would fill a gap. No one had traveled the world with the idea of describing its skies. Until now, voyagers had looked up to locate the North Star or Ursus Major, for navigational purposes. Or, worse (from a scientific perspective), they had looked up and described the sunset, proving (especially to the ladies) that beneath their tough explorer's exterior lay the soul of a poet. No one, as yet, had set off to look at the infinitely changeable landscape of the clouds, in all the latitudes, over every ocean and every mountain. That was what he, Richard Abercrombie, would do, no matter how long it took him. With his waxed moustache and impeccable white linen suit, he was not a man who changed course.

Abercrombie's voyage initially was little different from those of other world travelers. He had the usual sorts of adventures: His suitcase and some binoculars had been stolen in Bordeaux; he'd endured a storm in the Bay of Biscay, during which, he noted with particular pride, he had felt not the slightest seasickness; there had been an eight-hour stopover

in Lisbon, where he'd tried a number of wines, some of them
not at all bad; in Cap Blanc off West Africa he'd been surprised how cold it was, given that this was after all Africa, and
Africa was supposed to be hot—and when he found an explanation for this curious phenomenon of nature he decided he
would note it down for the reader of *Seas and Skies of Several Latitudes.* He crossed most of Senegal without paying much attention to it, having noted that the coastline reminded him
of Spain's, which had not been to his taste. Soon enough he
came in view of the Cape of Good Hope, where he stayed for
a while, as he was quite interested in diamonds and how they
were cut; he purchased a rough diamond of quite large size;
he cited the boasts of hunters. He noted how unhealthy the
climate in Madagascar and the Island of Mauritius was, and
that the numbers of dead were too great for immediate burial, and they gave off the most horrific smell; he compared
the vegetation in Mauritius to that of Fiji. He visited some
sugarcane factories; he found the workers filthy and dishon-
est; the bananas, on the other hand, were delectable. In the
Indian Ocean he attempted to predict weather patterns,
with moderate success. In January of 1890 he reached Ade-
laide Bay in Australia, deciding that the harbor of Rio de
Janeiro in Brazil possessed greater majesty, of that there
could be no doubt, the opinions of the locals notwithstand-
ing. He traveled north toward Ceylon, where he witnessed a
tea harvest. He pushed on to Madras, from which he traveled
overland to the Himalayas; there he bought a prayer wheel and
compared the surrounding mountains to the Alps. In March
of that year he reached the Indonesian archipelago. Having
tasted the local delicacy, swallows' nests, he determined that

they were of three varieties: The black nest was of the most inferior quality and sold for five shillings per pound in Hong Kong; the white nest was more prized, and contained neither feathers nor waste but only white saliva and swallow coagulation—they cost ten pounds; and the red nest was somewhere in the middle. He was invited to taste all three varieties, as prepared in a soup; he agreed to try the white. Accompanied by some locals, Abercrombie went fishing for trepangs, which are long black sea slugs you dive down and collect off the bottom. You slice them down the middle and wash out the insides, and then you place them in the sun to dry. Abercrombie ate them with finely cut slices of beef, and noted their taste to be somewhere between that of cockscomb and beef tongue; in any case they were quite delicious and he ate several helpings, to the amusement of the locals who served them to him (sea cucumbers were believed to enhance virility).

Finally, in April 1890, Abercrombie reached the kingdom of Sarawak, situated on the Island of Borneo's northwest coast. Here for the first time did he start keeping a full journal, written in the large green notebook. So far as we know, it remains the only volume to have survived the voyage. His writing style is similar to that in his published works—dry and matter-of-fact. Yet here, in Borneo, everything changed.

During the early part of April 1890, Abercrombie became acquainted with the British consulate in Sarawak. The consul, a man named Jones, was a seasoned colonial administrator. He had spent thirty years as a diplomat in the Far East, never experiencing a single run-in or set-to with the local potentate; he had never sat anyone in the wrong place at a dinner party, and indeed had never been guilty of even the slightest error in protocol. Jones was a portly man, as elegant and vain as a bauble. With an arsenal of fifty well-honed anecdotes, adaptable to every situation imaginable in a consul's life, he slipped from one sinecure to the next, somehow managing to avoid the more challenging postings. Jones was exceptionally vigilant about essentials; his dinners were faultless, and afterward he always offered round the finest cigars, which he managed to protect from the tropical humidity. For twelve years he had set his sights on Bali. Jones would die in his sleep of a heart attack the following year, without once having been struck by the sheer futility of his life. His wife would resent him for dying so early and so vulgarly. His heart stopped beating at ten o'clock in the evening, and she didn't return home until eight the following morning, by which point Jones's body had begun to leak all over the sheets, producing an odor that haunted his widow's nightmares—at least until she remarried a year later. But for the time being, Jones was still alive and his table open to guests. When Abercrombie set foot on the wharf at the port of Sandakan, Jones was there to welcome him.

Abercrombie accepted the consul's invitation to dine. This was an exceptional thing for him to do; he had become accomplished in the subtle art of dodging precisely such invitations, under the pretext of a slight illness or last-minute change in travel plans or something involving quarantine. When he disembarked at Sandakan, his reputation—that of a misanthropic genius on a mysterious mission into a vital new field of inquiry—preceded him. In the noisy, tongue-wagging colonial world, Abercrombie's silence was simply thunderous. He accepted Jones's invitation because he felt the need to take stock of what had happened in the months since his departure from England. To his own great surprise, Abercrombie was finding that the farther he got from the limited circles of scientific organizations, of libraries and congresses, the less and less interesting his mission was. He pursued it single-mindedly but without the zeal he had felt initially. Perhaps what he needed, he decided, was to strengthen his ties with human society. Here he was standing on a noisy wharf, and someone had been talking with him for some minutes. All the while, he was making murmurs of approbation and all those other noncommittal little social gestures. This fat, well-attired little man was talking to him animatedly and

had invited him to dinner. He accepted, pocketing the calling card of the consul, whose face flushed with pleasure as he
beetled off to inform his wife of the news, before this fierce
and austere man might change his mind.

Abercrombie hired a rickshaw to take him to his hotel.
He let his mind wander in a refreshing bath; for months he
had been tumbling like a pebble from one nation to the next
and in the process become polished. He had seen so many
different kinds of men, women, and children; so many local
habits of the most surprising sort; so much outrageous dress;
so many outlandish tastes. However, behind the picturesque
diversity of all these cultures lay something deeper, something even more human, and it exceeded the basic model
supplied by his concept of *Homo Britannicus,* of Civilized Man,
even of Man. He had fumbled his way upon the tiny inde-
structible core of humanity.

The dinner Abercrombie attended that very evening was
representative of life in the colonies: The flotsam and jetsam
of the Western world had washed up at the table of Consul
Jones. Against all expectation, nonetheless, he had an excellent time. The colonial dregs were not more or less worthy of
sympathetic interest than the Australian aborigines who had
honored him by reciting the unending list of their ancestors
and relations; nor more or less than the Mongol peasants
who had served him spoiled milk and a stew that contained
god-knows-what but which turned out to be quite delicious.
At the table, naturally, were some hunters, who completed a
consul's tropical menagerie. One was James Alfred Crooks, a
large man, rose-hued and blond. He had plunged a promi-
nent Wisconsin family into grief in a drunken brawl and thus

been forced to leave his native America, or at least so said a breathless woman sitting next to Abercrombie in hushed tones. Crooks's best friend was Dr. Benjamin Walker, a small, rotund man who sat directly across from him. He was as pink as a leg of ham and his pendulous cheeks were testaments to the vigor of his appetite. Walker was as talkative as Crooks was taciturn. This colorful duo had won invitations to the finest tables in Southeast Asia; they always had a story to offer over dessert, one that would make the women gasp and the men chuckle. These were redoubtable hunters, consulted whenever a tiger hunt was being contemplated, or a safari being organized for some high-level functionary visiting the area while on a tour of inspection.

One could always count upon Walker and Crooks to earn their board. This particular evening they were armed with some unusually striking tales, indeed almost outlandish ones. Walker was waxing loquaciously about the cow elephant that had sought revenge when they'd killed her baby; and about how his friend Alfred had been attacked by a giant alligator; and about how, once, while aiming at a bird of really remarkable plumage he had found himself unable to pull the trigger. Crooks supported his friend's performance with a solemn nodding of the head and an assortment of approving grunts. Abercrombie admitted to them that he'd never been on this kind of hunt before. Well, he needed to say no more. One was immediately proposed for his benefit. By the time coffee and brandy were being served in the salon, under the watchful eyes of Jones, eyes watering with pleasure at the thought of how really successful this dinner had turned out to be, Walker and Crooks continued their performance,

showering Abercrombie with recommendations and prom-
ises: about how if the fates smiled upon them they might help
him bag a species of local peccary, a short-haired boar sometimes known to attack those hunting it; some birds of paradise that it would be difficult to stuff, given how quickly
everything rotted in the dense jungle underbrush; and various species of deer. Abercrombie asked if they might come
across tigers. Walker and Crooks laughed heartily at this,
joined by the consul. The ladies asked the reason for their
merriment. Because you see, Crooks informed them, there
are no tigers on Borneo, not unless they happened to have
swum over from China. With this riotously funny pleasantry
the consul's wife signaled that the women would now proceed to the tables for cards.

In the smoking room, Abercrombie condescended to explain the spicier aspects of developments in meteorological
theory to the consul, who was alarmed by complications of
any sort. They all went out on the terrace to take the air;
before them floated, just above the line of administrative
buildings belonging to the customs office, a single, elongated
cloud. Abercrombie was surprised by not knowing exactly
how to classify it. The cloud's altitude suggested one type and
its form another. He wondered whether it wouldn't after all
be necessary to formulate a classification of nighttime clouds,
as the Spaniard Figueroa had suggested at a congress in Rome
in 1885. How right he had been, felt Abercrombie, to have re-
newed his contacts with his fellow being. The farther away
from England he got, the more his enthusiasm for scientific
investigation had with increasing cruelty abandoned him. He
took his leave and walked slowly toward the port and to his

hotel. Behind him the consul was being congratulated by his wife in their bedchamber, something that had not happened for quite some time. They had *had* Abercrombie, and in their rarefied circles that fact might be used as leverage to obtain a diplomatic post in a less dreary place than this industrial port where, for many years, woodblocks of no great value had been loaded—away from this forgotten backwater where out of sheer idleness Jones had spent nights in the bordellos so as not to die from boredom.

Abercrombie returned alone, but the walk rekindled a little of his scientific curiosity. Lifting his eyes skyward, he noted with a certain degree of melancholy that other clouds he had never before seen had gathered over his head. He had a strange dream that night: The last cloud in the world— enormous and black—was following him across the sands of a desert in reproachful silence.

PART III

The Abercrombie Protocol

Somewhat curiously, never once in the face of this liquid
or aerial magic did I mourn the absence of man.
—*Baudelaire*

On April 17, 1890, a small steam-powered launch carrying three white men and two natives chugged along the northwest coast of Borneo. It was the finest vessel to be found in the region and moved through the water with ease, but it still looked decrepit; the climate prematurely ages everything. At the tiller was Dr. Benjamin Walker, guiding the boat in a straight line, parallel to the coast, on water that was placid, dark, and appeared lifeless. As they were leaving the port they had admired the homes of the white inhabitants. Then they had passed the native shacks, where indistinct garlands of children moved and the elderly sat motionless on benches. Eventually they had left behind all signs of human habitation. Only twenty minutes out of port and there was nothing but a partially collapsed floating dock and the remains of a building rotting among the vegetation. James Crooks sat in the bow, near Abercrombie, who was sketching, and told him that these ruins were a rubber-tree concession abandoned the previous year. The owner had hanged himself at the start of the rainy season, and in less than two weeks the plantation had been devoured by jungle; in a year you wouldn't be able to distinguish anything at all. Crooks pointed out where the machinery had been housed, and the workers' sleeping quarters, and all the other remnants of civilization. Abercrombie saw nothing but endless lines of mangroves, silent as posts, gray and gallowslike.

A little further along, Walker indicated a point along a dark and seemingly unbroken line of tree trunks, announcing that here lay the mouth of the Sapu Gaya River. Abercrombie squinted but saw no break in the line of trees. He was determined not to act like a disappointed tourist, though by this point he had decided that the jungle was irredeemably grim. Nonetheless, he had also to concede that it matched the descriptions in written accounts he had read. Clearly, it was one thing to read, as a child, about the impenetrability of tropical forests and something altogether different to see firsthand the dark curtain of trees while inhaling the sickening odor of warm iodine and putrefying silt. Only at the last possible moment, when the boat was heading straight at the shore, did Abercrombie finally perceive a gap and with it the mouth of the Sapu Gaya, toward which Crooks was guiding them with such assurance. It would be necessary to find a mooring; anchorage was impossible. The water seemed so slow as to be nearly stagnant; black bubbles churned sluggishly in their wake.

The lightweight, six-man canoe they took from here up the river was highly maneuverable. Within three quarters of an hour the two natives, who did the rowing, had steered it into a small tributary whose entire length was jutted with giant, half-submerged tree trunks. The canoe, brand-new, seemed eerily out of place in the nearly prehistoric landscape. One could hear the discordant cry of peacocks; various species of grasshopper and cricket whose names Walker proudly offered up in Latin as well as in the local dialect; the screech of the great hornbill, which sounds like nothing else on earth; the insistent hum of flies; the deafening shrill of mosquitoes; and a deep rumble from deep below the surface of the dark water. For the first time in his life, Abercrombie was confronting nature in its most obscene, vehement, and luxuriant incarnation: The jungle. Even more disorienting than these noises was its complete absence of human cadence. The jungle trumpeted its own laws, indifferent to anyone who would explore it. In the forests of Europe and particularly those in England—all of them located near towns—animals had learned to grow silent at the approach of man, and to flee this creature that killed without the justification of survival. The tranquility of the countryside was the tangible sign of man's reign of terror.

Passage up this tributary of the Sapu Gaya became more difficult. The muddy bottom rose closer to the surface and weighty, nightmarish sludge coiled behind the canoe. They had to hack with machetes at the vegetation, which was closing in above them. Eventually they edged their way up onto a sandy outcropping in a small pool whose water, compared to the silt-heaving currents they had navigated until now, was stunningly clear. They came to rest against the trunk of a large tree that by all appearances had very recently been struck by lightning. Here was where they would venture out on foot. The three men set off into the jungle, following behind the natives, who cleared a trail. Crooks, snorting like a bull, explained to Abercrombie that a half-hour's walk from here was a series of clearings where they would be able to hunt at their leisure. Now that he was actually in the jungle Abercrombie couldn't suppress his disappointment. While in the canoe, he had thought that experiencing the jungle directly would change everything, but walking through it was no less disillusioning. He ground his teeth in vexation as they moved with desperate slowness, stumbling over rotted logs. They were bathed in a darkness that was nearly total, and sticky, and unformed. Around them were unidentifiable flora and the cries of animals that obstinately refused to reveal themselves. The sun was shining seventy-five feet over their heads, above the canopy of branches and vines in which most of Borneo's wildlife, apart from a few frogs and toads, chose as their habitat. Abercrombie felt keenly now that the jungle was a desert. You couldn't see more then ten feet ahead in the tangle of vegetation. Taking a single step involved first hacking a swathe. Three times, one of the obliging guides pointed a finger toward a rare spot of light, to show the white men a remarkable specimen of some species or other, and each time Abercrombie saw nothing. With customary American forthrightness, the hunter made matters worse by chatting brightly about everything they were not seeing. The upper strata of the jungle were as splendid as the lower were lifeless, he explained. At this very moment, a hundred feet above their heads, among the tops of the trees, were orchids and butterflies, mangoes and durians swollen by sunshine. Monkeys and large snakes lived there. It was possible to reach these heights, but forging a vertical trail would take several days and require a team of seasoned natives, as well as all the equipment necessary for securing a post at the summit. It would have to be left for another day.

After twenty minutes of painful progress, they extracted themselves from one last thicket and abruptly found themselves in a long clearing. It took several minutes for Abercrombie's eyes to adjust to the sunlight, which ruled supreme here. They were in a kind of elliptical vegetative amphitheater. High, lush green grass sloped gradually down to a brook; it caressed their bare forearms as they walked through it.

Abercrombie approached what seemed to be a flowering bush when suddenly it seemed to fly apart into the air—it had been covered with small blue butterflies. The cries of animals were muffled by the thickness of the undergrowth. A bird with a compact body and flame-colored plumage flew lazily off to his right; it seemed unaffected by their presence. Dr. Walker turned around and gestured to Abercrombie to freeze. With impressive elegance and agility, Crooks raised the muzzle of his rifle, which he had been cradling in his right arm. Without seeming to aim, in one motion he stiffened his arm and his shoulder and pulled the trigger. The bird was forty feet in front of them, about to alight on some foliage. Not knowing what game he would be shooting at that day, Crooks had decided to charge the rifles with large-caliber bullets. He scored a direct hit: The creature exploded into a brilliant shower of feathers and bloody tatters. The sound of the gunshot ripped through the jungle and for a moment everything went eerily silent. Abercrombie still had not moved. He watched the last of the feathers dancing in the air. The beauty of the spot in which they were standing struck him once more. One could almost convince oneself that nothing had just happened, yet a deepening feeling of shame spread through his body. Crooks chattered loudly while reloading his rifle. Walker, who had walked to the edge of the clearing, returned. Abercrombie was bathed in sweat. Noting how pale the meteorologist looked, Crooks suggested that perhaps Professor Abercrombie might like to refresh himself near the brook while he and Walker ventured on to another clearing, a bit further along, a place the natives assured them offered the perfect spot in which to hunt for bigger game. Abercrombie gladly acceded to this. Within a few minutes the natives had fashioned some purple-veined ferns into a sort of primitive but comfortable litter with a sloping canopy. The sun blazed over their heads. They told Abercrombie to fire his rifle in the event he needed help. One of the natives gave him some slices of fruit. Then they moved off to the sound of crashing branches until reabsorbed by the jungle. After eating the fruit slices, which were delicious, Abercrombie decided to lie down beneath the cloudless sky. Occasionally he rose to his elbows to gaze again at the meadow, the sparkling water of the brook, the random ballet of tiny insects in the light. It was so beautiful here. One might die in peace. He thought about nothing at all. He was almost happy.

$Time\ crept\ lazily$ in the clearing. Abercrombie had dozed off, trusting as a child. It was impossible that such a place could conceal anything dangerous. Gradually, a strange sensation started bringing him back toward awareness. Without opening his eyes he could tell that the sun had moved: He sensed its joyous burn on his right arm, which was spread out on the grass. He kept his eyes closed for the sheer pleasure of anticipating what it would be like to open them again to a world in which, at least for a while, men did not exist. He opened his eyes. The others had had the foresight to settle him within the confines of a gap in the vegetation, three steps away from where the seemingly motionless brook that ran through the clearing widened out into a pool of water. The curious sensation that had roused him, a tingling around his neck and on his legs and arms, grew sharper, until finally it forced him to rise slowly to his feet, still more curious than alarmed, to seek its cause.

Gazing around the clearing, he rubbed his neck, and his hand made contact with something viscous. It was a leech.

Travelers to the equatorial zones were familiar with these parasites. Abercrombie knew he should not attempt to pull it off, as doing so might result in an infected wound. From a pocket in his linen vest he drew out a smooth chrome cylinder and from it extracted a pinch of tobacco. Using saliva he moistened a few sprigs in the palm of his hand, then reached back and rubbed it on the creature. The leech released its hold and fell. Abercrombie crushed it thoroughly under his boot heel. His ordeal wasn't over. From beneath the soft linen of his trousers he could make out small, black, slow-moving protuberances. His legs were covered with leeches. Others were moving through the soft, pastel-colored grass, crawling toward him as if he were some great reservoir of blood. Abercrombie removed his clothes. He was forced to use up all his tobacco. When he had finally dealt with the last one, he sought refuge on a large rock that jutted fortuitously over the pool of clear water and lay beyond the reach of these creatures. The black basalt was hot under his feet. He moved his fingers over his back—forcing him into contortions—until satisfied he was free of them. He found himself smiling at the spectacle he would offer the others upon their return. Then he inspected every inch of his outfit, spreading his clothes out on the rock to dry. He crouched down on his haunches, his bare skin registering the smallest variations of breeze. At some point he lifted his head and discovered that he was not alone.

From the other side of the pool a creature was looking at him. It was a large monkey. The light breeze carried the animal's musky scent directly into Abercrombie's face, a breath of the wild. He felt no fear whatever, didn't think of reaching for his gun. Looking at him from across the brook was a *Mías Pappan,* as the natives called them, a member of the largest of the orangutan family. The creature did not move. Abercrombie suppressed a smile. He seemed to recall that a number of animal species perceived the display of teeth as threatening. This was an adult female, for around her neck and clinging to her long hair was a baby with a tiny wizened face, sleeping with its mouth open. The orangutan examined Abercrombie with great seriousness. Her hands were posed on the edge of the pool before her, scarcely ten feet's distance from him. Her eyes were set deep beneath two leathery black patches, which were liked malformed cheekbones; her face was crisscrossed with scars. At first Abercrombie held her gaze but then quickly averted his eyes, for she was giving him the kind of look that is directed at you and yet which goes through you: the way an ape looks. And in the eyes of a beast that had never before come across those of a man, there was absolutely nothing the slightest bit savage.

Much later, when Abercrombie no longer felt competent to judge his contemporaries, or to read his journal, or to debate issues of the day; when he was no longer the man of science he was thought to be; and when he would wonder what had happened to him, seeking in his past the source of his transformation, he would invariably be drawn back to this very moment in the clearing, and yet without really knowing why, without comprehending and also without mourning the fact that he didn't comprehend.

During the mere seconds this confrontation lasted, a flash of memory came to Abercrombie. It involved some aborigines he had photographed in the region around Perth in southwest Australia. A colleague and fellow member of the Royal Society had offered to show him the area's curiosities; among these were an aboriginal couple he had taken in, out of charity and scientific interest. They were the last survivors of a tribe of farmers pushed out of Perth, where they had lived for ages; a smallpox epidemic had wiped out the rest of their clan. Abercrombie had sat with them on a hollowed-out log at the back courtyard of the scientist's home. Later, while the woman hoed a scraggly field, the man sang for his host. Abercrombie had taken photographs of them. On the reverse of the image he had noted the obvious similarities between the couple and lesser-evolved primates. Now he remembered the man and the woman and their hospitality, and he felt a violent surge of shame.

Time resumed its course; the noise of the jungle was returning, as if from some great distance. The orangutan made a vague movement that was abbreviated because, suddenly, her right eye spasmed and was covered by a growing black stain; a second later the sound of the gunshot reached Abercrombie's ears. Without seeming to react, the animal fell to her knees, noiselessly. The second bullet passed through her partly opened mouth, rocking her head forward. In silence, the animal fell to the grass onto its left side. Her baby started to wail, its cry joined by those of hundreds of invisible animals.

When Abercrombie turned slowly to locate the source of the shot, he saw Crooks, crouching, his rifle positioned in the fork of a tree several hundred feet away. The hunter stood up and began walking through the bright sunshine toward Abercrombie, his rifle cradled in his arms, moving with the assured gait of the marksman who knows he has struck his mark; his rifle sight gave off bright shivers of reflected light. Now he was next to Abercrombie and waiting, quite visibly expecting to be complimented for his accomplishment. No praise was forthcoming. Unperturbed, Crooks handed his rifle to Abercrombie and began to head to the other side of the stream, where the indistinct orange heap lay. The tiny offspring was trying in vain to rouse it from immobility. First the baby had shaken its mother's breast, then pulled on its fur. Abercrombie could not bear to look at the body whose weight was settling into the grass and releasing its heat into the ambient air, losing the inimitable suppleness of a living thing. Crooks leaned over the dead female and rubbed his hands on its fur, then extended them to the baby, which had sought refuge behind its mother's corpse. The animal immediately leapt into the hunter's arms. The sound of the snap was barely discernible. Crooks placed the tiny body atop that of its mother. He turned toward Abercrombie to explain that without its mother it wouldn't have survived for three hours. Abercrombie knew that he was right. Then, remarkably, Crooks had the sense to keep his mouth shut. He resisted recounting to Abercrombie colorful tales about how *Mías Pappans* had attacked hunters or ripped the arm of a native right off or spent twenty years seeking revenge for the killing of one of their young. Instead, thrown off by Abercrombie's silence, Crooks said not a thing. That was probably the reason Abercrombie didn't kill him.

Doctor Walker entered the clearing, drawn by the rifle shots. He brought Abercrombie back to more prosaic matters by handing him his undergarments and white-linen trousers. Abercrombie dressed. The natives talked excitedly. Sensing that generous tips might be forthcoming, they congratulated the white men warmly. This was Crooks's and Walker's favorite part of the hunt: the narrative. Crooks related to Walker what had happened. Walker pressed for more details. Crooks supplied what he could, guessing at a few things and making up the rest. They turned toward Abercrombie, who was now dressed. It was his turn to join the game, to offer up his version of the sequence of events as precisely as he could—from the sudden fatigue that had overcome him, to the leeches, to the confrontation with the beast. He did so, mechanically. Along the hard smooth surface of Abercrombie's monument to himself as a civilized man, a long crack had started to form. For now he chose to ignore it, for fear that the whole edifice might crumble. After twenty minutes he even felt on the verge of agreeing with his two companions that the whole episode had really been rather comical: the naked man of science facing the hairy beast. Crooks and Walker were in ecstasy.

Crooks proposed they take photographs to commemorate the event. The local newspaper was sure to run them. He and Walker begged Abercrombie to unpack his equipment. Sniffing around the animal, Walker was already outlining in his head the article that he would submit to the *Indonesian Chronicle,* burnishing a few deeply felt yet appropriate sentiments. Abercrombie, for his part, regretted having brought his photographic apparatus, but decided it was easier to go along with these imbeciles; resisting them was too exhausting. He obediently set up his tripod and camera.

Meanwhile, Crooks, knife in hand, went to work; he was experienced at constructing these hunting tableaux. Picking up the dead baby he tossed it as far as he could; it was hardly presentable. The tiny corpse disappeared among the deep grass, though its location was soon enough indicated by a dark cloud of insects. Abercrombie willed himself not to look at the spot. In two hours all that would remain would be bones, teeth, and cartilage. With darkness a vulture would arrive, or perhaps one of a variety of rodents, and crunch the little bones to extract their marrow. As for its mother, Walker happily confirmed that it was quite a beautiful specimen, roughly four and a half feet from head to toe; the arms were exceptionally powerful, even in a species known for arm strength; from fingertip to fingertip it measured 8.2 feet. It weighed somewhere around two hundred pounds. In Sandakan, Walker also functioned as an undertaker, and on behalf of his esteemed scientific colleague, he said, would be only too happy to prepare the scene. With a piece of vine he tied the animal's jaws shut, then cleaned off what remained of the eyeball, which had dribbled down the cheekbone, and stuffed the empty socket with some twigs he first crushed and then rolled into the right shape. After that he broke the animal's stiffened arms with his rifle butt, to give them greater flexibility. He propped the body up from behind by means of a stake that he had gone to the edge of the forest to find and then whittled, and faced her forward, making clever use of some branches to brace up her arms. He also broke the animal's toes to get them to close like fists. The result was a ferocious-looking beast positioned in a most striking and photogenic manner. Of course Abercrombie had to stand behind the orangutan. Crooks found it amusing to kneel on the dead creature's right side, holding its wrist the way you would hold a toddler's you had taken out for a walk. Walker took the first photograph, then he and Crooks swapped places. Finally it was finished. Abercrombie hoped that the natives might claim the orangutan's remains as sacred to their culture, and engage in some kind of ceremony to mark the passage of this great creature. They didn't feel any such impulse. Essentially vegetarians, they had no interest in the animal's muscular flesh, which was both inedible and worth nothing in the markets.

However, at Walker's orders they did skin the orangutan, using long curved knives sharp as razorblades, and with a rapidity Abercrombie found disconcerting. They were careful not to sever the animal's hands and feet. They started a fire next to the corpse. Abercrombie thought it odd that the flayed body wasn't grotesquely bloody. After that they put the fire out and dragged the remains further away. The scramble was on: Every variety of insect and tiny flesh-eater flew, jumped, and crawled toward the pink heap in the grass. To keep it supple enough for taxidermy, Walker rolled the bloody pelt of the *Mías Pappan* in a briny solution, the ingredients for which he always carried in his haversack (the unbreakable habit of an amateur taxidermist, he explained). After rinsing it and brushing it, he rolled it again in the solution. There were two hours of daylight left; it was time to leave the clearing. Before they plunged back into the jungle, Abercrombie turned his head slightly, and at the edge of his field of vision he could sense where the two dark spots lay.

They made their way back to the canoe, and then to the launch, floating lazily on the brackish river. Out on open water, by the light of a storm lamp, Abercrombie pretended to write in his notebook so that he might be left alone. The thought of offering up a prayer to the great ape came to him. He dismissed the idea as absurd. He offered up the prayer nonetheless and was barely finished with it by the time they had reached the calm waters of Sandakan Harbor. Crooks suggested that the three of them proceed directly to the consul's residence for a drink; it was that time of day, after all. Abercrombie told them that he wanted first to return to his hotel in order to develop the images that would substantiate the account of the day's events they would offer that same evening in the presence of the consul, with whom they had agreed to dine. They arranged to meet in Abercrombie's hotel lobby at half past eight. Walker and Crooks hurried off; they had barely enough time to change.

At half past eight Walker and Crooks presented themselves at the lobby of the hotel, the only hotel in the port;
they were wearing their finest hunting outfits and thinking
with tenderness about their great new friend Richard Abercrombie, partly because they were already drunk in the way
that colonial men get drunk, and partly because they owed to
him perhaps the most sensational hunting story of their long
careers. Half an hour later, Abercrombie still had not appeared. With a heavy tread Crooks climbed the stairs and
knocked at his door. No response. They learned from a porter
that the guest in Room 16 had checked out and headed down
to the port some hours before. And indeed, right after they
had left him on the street, Abercrombie had gone up to his
room, packed his bags, and booked immediate passage on a
Chinese junk that would take him to the next port, twelve
miles south of Sandakan. When Walker and Crooks reached
the dock, a Malay fisherman pointed out the tiny red dot on
the horizon, slowly heading south. Walker most deeply regretted the loss of the photographs in the baggage of that
spoilsport old hypocrite. Crooks had been deprived of the
only evidence of his truly exceptional shot. Still, the two
friends set off for Consul Jones's home at a brisk pace and
with light hearts, for they realized that Abercrombie's absence left them free to tell their own versions of what happened. The dinner was more than a success; it was a triumph.

The following day, a Sunday, Crooks helped his friend
stuff the orangutan. Standing erect, the monster, its left fist
thumping its chest, appeared to be threatening an imaginary
assailant, baring its teeth, its raised right hand poised to strike.
A month later, Dr. Walker received, without accompanying

note, a complete set of the photographs that had been taken in the clearing. The *Indonesian Chronicle* agreed to publish a written account of the event along with an illustrative supplement. Crooks's and Walker's social standing achieved its zenith. Abercrombie, meanwhile, was far away.

Inside the green-covered journal Abercrombie left behind, Virginie told Kumo, were the factual details of the
story she had just recounted. What it did not contain was his
commentary. Abercrombie never expressed his emotions regarding any of the incidents he recorded, however compro-
mising to him personally. Crammed among the pages were
cabin tickets and dried flowers. There were also copies of the
photographs taken in the clearing. Virginie held them out
to Kumo, who took them eagerly. They were more or less
alike, these prints on thick cardboard; the fixing solutions
had frothed a little, and the edges assumed that ethereal air
of things whose passage through time hasn't been easy. The
orangutan is posed at the edge of the jungle. In the background are the massive roots of an enormous tree, roots so
massive that you can't distinguish them from the trunk; they
look like flying buttresses. The orangutan's one eye appears
to be focused on some distant point beyond the frame of the
photograph; the creature has the melancholy, surprised expression of murdered innocence. Behind it two men are stand-

ing. Kumo had no difficulty recognizing Abercrombie. The other, his chest puffed out, has the triumphant look of a Boy Scout raised on whole milk and pancakes soaked in butter and syrup; his smile is that of a bully. Next to him Abercrombie appears tiny, almost Asian. His hairline is receding but he has combed his hair straight back in the manner of a man unconcerned by such things. He holds his rifle by the barrel, as if it were a violin. He doesn't seem to be looking at anything in particular. His thick moustache obscures his face, but somehow this makes him seem more rather than less vulnerable. Kumo thought that the orangutan looked like a pirate who had been taken prisoner, and Abercrombie like one of his crew.

Evening fell on Paris. Virginie departed. Kumo continued to look at the photographs. Members of his staff eventually came in, surrounded him, just as they had every evening since the accident, lifted his chair, and carried him down to his room. The night nurse washed and powdered Kumo, then slipped him into the clean sheets of a freshly made bed.

After April 17, 1890, Richard Abercrombie ceased taking photographs of clouds. The Chinese junk deposited him on the southern part of the Island of Borneo; from there he booked passage on a commercial ship. Six days after the incident in the clearing he was in Bali. Neither the tobacco nor the sea air had prevented the leech bites from becoming infected. The suppurating sores made wearing clothes too painful. One evening, wearing only a simple sarong, he went to see a Chinese healer who had been recommended to him. The treatment prescribed was, thought Abercrombie, ludicrously complex. The healer gave him five pots of a white ointment and instructed him to massage it into his skin for five evenings in succession at exactly the same hour. Abercrombie took up residence in a hotel on the port, where he ran no risk of running into someone who might invite him to dine or go on an expedition. All the non-European races seemed to be represented in this dank place, whose owner, for reasons mysterious to Abercrombie, had named the Regent. It was in a neighborhood bustling with pimps, opium dealers, child slavers, and temple pillagers. The locale where he was told he might obtain a massage was quite obviously a bordello, but the bites were causing him such pain that he overcame his scruples. The mistress of the house showed him into a clean room where there was a tub of water and, on the floor, a large mat woven of coconut fiber. Abercrombie lay down on it. Soon a young woman entered; she was large and placid, her golden skin smooth. She straddled him and began gently to rub the ointment into the wounds of this odd client, who spoke to her in a rudimentary Javanese vocabulary. Abercrombie was forty-nine years old and still a virgin. He had not touched himself in thirteen years. Had the young woman made any sort of obscene overture there is little doubt he would have retreated back into his chastity and departed immediately. But she had known stranger clients than Abercrombie. She was surprised by nothing, and blessed with incomparable intuition when it came to matters of the flesh. Abercrombie's penis stiffened. He closed his eyes. Gently sliding her right foot up his thigh, she massaged his penis, and then moved her hands down his left leg. Her hands were so soft and so warm that Abercrombie never noticed when she started using her mouth.

The next evening, at the same hour, Abercrombie returned and requested her services again. He was made to wait a little. Then the ritual recommenced. He gave into it with a slight air of detachment. This time it was her sex and not her mouth that enveloped his. Crouched over him, she slowly moved the muscles of her stomach. Immediately he was struck by a wave of pleasure. Afterward she rubbed his wounds and finished his massage. Abercrombie left the three remaining pots of ointment with the mistress of the house and went back to sleep at the Regent Hotel.

By the time the last pot was emptied, all traces of the wounds had disappeared. But every evening for the next few months, Abercrombie went and lay down on the mat. He knew nothing about lovemaking, but he was an avid student.

By virtue of spending evenings in a bordello and days sleeping in his hotel room, he got out of the habit of looking at clouds. The monsoon season was approaching. He went one last time to visit the young woman. To thank her for everything she had done for him, he purchased her from the bordello's mistress. She was free, he told her. She would return to her village, which was some distance from Bali, lie to her family about what she had been doing, and, eventually, marry. On this last occasion they were together Abercrombie brought his photography equipment. He wanted to memorialize this young woman whose name he did not know. Perhaps she misinterpreted his intentions; perhaps he insisted that she pose in this manner. Whichever the case, she undid her loincloth, lay down on the mat, and with her hands spread wide her labia. Abercrombie set up his camera and took the first of a whole new kind of photograph.

Virginie spent the remainder of the summer cataloguing and annotating Abercrombie's journal on Kumo's behalf. After Borneo, Abercrombie abandoned international meteorological guidelines. He was making up for lost time in the inexhaustible if repetitive domain of physical love. In September he was in Papua New Guinea; at the start of 1892 he returned to New Zealand. He went back to Australia, moving northward up its eastern coast toward the Tonga Islands. As no women were available in Tonga, he went to Japan. Everywhere he went he photographed women. He would start by taking up residence in the largest port cities, and then as soon as possible seek out the places sailors frequented. He scouted around for the best brothels and set to work. He noted everything he did and everything done to him, and how many times. His resolve and meticulousness were unswerving.

Virginie was beginning to think about life after Kumo. He had raised the subject; it was understood that he would make a second attempt. He told her that he wanted to help her. She found it easier to determine what she didn't want to do rather than what she did. All she knew for certain was that she couldn't go back to the library.

It was Richard Abercrombie, Jr., who found a temporary but lucrative solution. The September issue of the journal of the International Meteorological Association featured a long interview with him in which he suggested—offering no specifics—that the legendary *Protocol* contained a very particular sort of photograph and drawing. Within weeks he had offers from publishers everywhere. With Virginie's agreement, he settled upon a fairly new American house that specialized in large-format and very expensive books of scientific interest; it was financed by a pharmaceutical company. At the end of October, Richard and Virginie cosigned a contract. She would work on preparing an edition of the *Abercrombie Protocol.* She would also write an authorized portrait of Abercrombie for a large British trade house, a book whose principal focus would be illuminating the events recounted in his journal.

Kumo summoned his strength for one final effort. He invited the head of the library system that employed Virginie—the *sous-directeur's* boss—to come to Rue Lamarck at his earliest convenience. An hour later, *Monsieur le directeur's* arrival was announced. The man was trembling with excitement. Kumo met him in the most imposing of his offices on the second floor and got straight to the point. He was thinking of donating his papers, the fruit of so many years of labor, to an institution. Among these papers were notebooks containing his sketches, his designs, letters from famous clientele, and works from fashion colleagues and from artists.

Universities in America and Japan had been offering their archival services, he explained, but he had always rejected their overtures, waiting to find what he felt would be the right place for his papers, a place where they would be well cared for. He wondered whether *Monsieur le directeur* would be interested in running a foundation for haute couture, one that would involve managing the Kumo Foundation's activities and awarding grants to promising young designers. The director, naturally, was deeply interested. Kumo asked him to speak to his staff to draft an agreement. The director was indeed dazzled by the offer, but was also waiting for the catch; there had to be a catch. The couturier thanked the director for having supplied him with an assistant as remarkable as Virginie Latour. Mademoiselle Latour, continued Kumo, had proven uncommonly knowledgeable and adept in the field of meteorological literature. Therefore, he wondered whether she wasn't being underused in her current capacity at the library. He asked the director to keep him personally informed about two matters—the disposition of his private papers and more appropriate employment for Mademoiselle Latour. The director pledged himself on both counts.

When she was not with Kumo on Rue Lamarck, Virginie lived with Abercrombie in London, laboring away on his grandfather's journal and sketching out his biography. She was comfortable financially, very happy sexually, and thus able to devote her new reserves of spiritual energy to work, the greatest of human activities, finding joy in meeting challenges and absorbing new things. Exhaustion from such labor is delicious. In the mornings she worked on her bibliographical description of the *Protocol;* in the afternoon she documented Abercrombie's life. The publisher had suggested the transparently commercial *The Lord of the Clouds* as a title.

News of the scabrous nature of the *Protocol* was spreading well beyond the small circles of cloud enthusiasts. It was being rumored that the original itself might be put up for auction to coincide with the appearance of the *Protocol* and the biography. There would be author tours and signings, throughout Britain and then in the U.S., perhaps other places as well. Virginie would be sought after by universities, with their generous speaker fees. And if everything went well there would be a new position for her somewhere in Europe, one commensurate with her interests. *Monsieur le directeur* was seeing to this. For the moment, however, Virginie was struggling to understand the theories Abercrombie was laying out in his journal. This was not easy, for his approach differed from the conventions of his day.

By May of 1891, Abercrombie was no longer content with photographing women. At first he had been informal about his methodology, as the *Protocol* reflected. The photographs, which were glued to the middle of their respective page, were labeled simply with the subject's last and first name (aside from the first one), the location (most often region, sometimes with the subject's ethnicity), and the date the picture was taken. This part of the album contained the most explicit images of women, who are either standing or lying down. Their faces are visible, however. After a point Abercrombie began focusing only on the subject's midriff, which had the effect of dehumanizing the sexual organ, creating landscapes of pure flesh, lunar, as it were, or volcanic. Virginie had only examined her own sex once, when she was twelve, and doing so had involved contortions with a tiny mirror. Here, spread out before her in the emotionless light of photography, were scores of vaginas. Their diversity surprised her; no one looked exactly like any other. This must have been what struck Abercrombie as he made the transition from uncompromising chastity to indulger in veritable feasts of carnality. Rather than refer to *the* female sexual organ in the singular, Abercrombie henceforth used the plural.

Starting in May of 1891, the *Protocol* changed yet again: The space around the photographs became filled with notes, drawings, and sketches. At first these appeared tentative and a little haphazard, and then they became more assured, though also more untamed and free-flowing. Soon the photographs appeared on their own on right-hand pages; the facing page was taken up entirely by notes and drawings. Among them were what could only be described as doodles. They followed a pattern. Outlined by a delicate stroke that looked like the representation of a brain, each successive line became smaller and smaller, twisting themselves into knots so tight they seemed to vanish.

The text exhibited precisely the opposite tendency. From embryonic in size the words became more spread out and increasingly enigmatic. Virginie patiently recorded each one in alphabetical order in a notebook, taking note of their location and frequency. Terms such as "similitude," "origin," and "parallelism" proliferated. "It makes you think that the shock of sexuality had been too great for him," Virginie told Richard one Sunday, when, tired of leaning over these old pages, she had gone down to the kitchen for a bite to eat. "He had wanted to reassume control." Richard said nothing in reply— his habit when he disagreed with something. He loathed psychology, believing that one should never *explain* a person, under any circumstances, and that one couldn't tour an individual the way one could some historic monument. People should be left alone, even after they were dead. He was beginning to tire of Virginie; of that he also said nothing.

Virginie was gradually uncovering a theme running through the *Protocol's* sometimes feverish profusion. Abercrombie had tried to demonstrate that everything in the universe reverted to the same forms. The world consisted of recurring combinations of these forms. In a long entry dated May 1891 he called this "isomorphism," a term he underlined three times. Several pages written at the beginning of June were also devoted to this principle, which reflected what was taking shape within Abercrombie's mind. The entries were written in a steady hand, with the tranquil sense of purpose that saints share with fools. He was in northern Japan, on the island of Hokkaido.

Abercrombie first set himself up in a bungalow that also served as a tea house—a brothel, in other words—not far from the port of Kushiro on the southern coast of Hokkaido. In hot weather it was the place the city's notables came to pass the day. At the end of the summer of 1891, he received the money he had asked the Tokyo branch of his bank to wire him. With the money he purchased the long-term services of six women from the tea house next door and rented the former winter residence of a local lord. Abercrombie arrived before the first frost with his caravan of prostitutes and crates of supplies. The winter palace sat above the shoreline of the La Perouse Straits separating Hokkaido from the Russian island of Sakhalin. It was a traditional structure, flat and low, consisting of two floors, and built out of black stone. A long sloping roof covered a cozy bathing area, consisting of a steam bath, three tubs, and a relaxation room. A barn, which one reached by means of a covered path bordered by a gray hedge, housed a sufficient quantity of firewood. Here Abercrombie spent the winter with his women, each with her own particular odor. Their taste lifted his heart, and he spent long days with his head between their thighs, until his tongue and his lips were numb.

The long winter evenings were devoted to working on the *Protocol.* In a page dated November 25, 1891, Abercrombie made a graphite drawing of a human brain. Below it was another, slightly modified, and then another. And so it went, drawing by drawing, until, as Virginie noted, they evolved into the representation of a cloud of the *altocumulus* group. A second series of drawings, undated, could be found three pages ahead. This time the *altocumulus* cloud gradually assumed the elegant and elaborate folds of a woman's sex. From here until the end the *Protocol* contained exercises of this sort. Abercrombie was patiently marrying clouds and things, parts of the body and objects found in nature. Sometimes a shell would become transformed into a human ear, a river turn into the gnarled bark of an olive tree.

When he wasn't drawing, he was in bed with his women, engaged in an activity that was increasingly becoming a scientific exploration for him. He feasted upon their sex, noting the faint traces of blood and salt water; he often discovered a taste of sand or earth in the crease of their buttocks. He dutifully catalogued all the results. He would caress their thighs until he could no longer distinguish his hand from the curvature of the body he was caressing. Each prostitute had her own comfortable room, and he voyaged among them. The snow blotted out the dark outline of Sakhalin, along with the rest of the world. When fatigue so overwhelmed him that he couldn't sleep, Abercrombie went for walks along the shore, beneath the branches of pines bowed by the capricious winds off the straits. In nice weather he collected shells on the beach, shells whose shapes he thought remarkable. All shapes were remarkable. The nacreous irregularities of a shell or the sensual roll of a wave invariably reminded him of a woman's curves and iridescent skin. Abercrombie would return to the enclosed rooms by a small path made of flat stones wet from spray.

One day, to amuse him, one of the women took a roll of etchings from her travel trunk. They depicted both erotic scenes and landscapes, and though they were unimaginatively precise copies of Japanese and Chinese masters, Abercrombie immediately recognized their kinship. These artists had painted landscapes the way artists in Europe painted bodies; and they painted landscapes as if they were bodies. Nothing was detached, or demeaned, or left out. He had found the secret to it all waiting patiently for him: the connectedness of all shapes.

Winter drew to a close. From the beach, Abercrombie sometimes saw long gray silhouettes sliding along the waters. These were ships of war, flying the colors of far-off lands. Abercrombie regarded them with a critical eye, as he did all infractions of the rules of universal harmony. These war machines had hard lines, and their gray metal hulls, their bridges covered with gun turrets, were an abomination to the blue water of the straits, to the shades of sky, and to the pale sweetness of the sun. Sometimes the ships came so near to shore the sailors waved to him.

Virginie found a photograph of Abercrombie from his days in Japan. She didn't recognize him at first. His face seemed featureless. Some of the wrinkles on his forehead and cheeks, the tangible indicators of high-minded erudition, had been smoothed away. The eyes seemed lighter, contrasted by the weather-beaten skin. It was spring, and Abercrombie was spending more and more of his time on the beach, meditating on the passage of warships and commercial vessels, of which there were more and more. He watched them with a growing feeling of revulsion. The United States, the rising world power (increasingly it was American ships that passed through the straits), seemed the least harmonious culture of all. He could already sense that what would triumph in the world was a civilization—rigid, formidably efficient, spiritually demented, militaristic, and mercantile—which had extracted analogies to the Universe from two thousand years of thought, in order to select those laws that would prove useful for making nature subservient, and for serving Progress. Abercrombie remained, at heart, a snob. It was of no concern to him that people's lives were constantly being bettered due precisely to the rupture that defined Western civilization. Such was his old-school arrogance, and his limitation.

There were moments when Virginie grew bored with the man. Like all crazy people of his sort Abercrombie was fastidious and repetitive; the theoretician in him was sometimes tinged with the grotesque. Yet there was also something stubbornly touching and pathetic about him. She pursued his life. It was becoming easier for her now. Besides, when Abercrombie the philosopher exhausted her, Abercrombie the empiricist enchanted her. He had the bodies of small animals dried in order to determine exactly how much water they contained. He monitored how much water the prostitutes drank and then measured the quantity they expelled. To advance the cause of science he devised erotic games, such as flavoring the water he made the women drink and then positioned himself beneath them and tasted their urine, to ascertain whether the anise, cardamom, or vanilla had passed through. He believed that he had established the basis of a new science. In May 1892, a fellow Englishman, a geologist, arrived in this remote part of the world. Abercrombie received him politely. The man handed Abercrombie a package wrapped in waxed cloth and tied up with string. Inside was six months of correspondence. Abercrombie opened only the letters from his bankers and learned that his personal fortune was still substantial.

Once the geologist had left, Abercrombie disbanded his *ménage*. It was time for him to visit other latitudes and to test his theories. Two months later he was in the Philippines, where he discovered with great interest a catamaran-like boat of Fijian origin. It consisted of two tapered hulls and a mainsail that was large yet still manageable. He learned to sail it in the Davao Gulf and became quite expert. Following his instructions, a local craftsman constructed one for him that was adapted to open-water navigation. At the front of each of the two hulls a trunk was installed and waterproofed; beneath the planks were containers of fresh water. Abercrombie's plan was to reach the more temperate zones under his own sail. It seemed unthinkable to him now that he would book passage on a ship, and be forced to arrive for dinner in the mess at the appointed hour, to find he had been seated between a retired military officer with a liver complaint and a grocer's widow.

He turned fifty in August of 1892, living half-naked under the sun out on the open water. At this very moment, in London, somber-looking gentlemen in evening dress were gravely greeting one another in the clubs and in learned societies and in the chambers of Parliament, places where they were enacting laws, expressing hypotheses, and drawing on pipes while commenting upon the latest cricket matches and horse races. He had once been such a man.

For months Abercrombie wandered the Pacific, without any particular destination and without haste, a king without a kingdom. The catamaran lived up to its designer's expectations, able to handle the strongest winds (though in this season they were not especially violent), and progressing under full sail. It was the perfect analogical vessel. As he passed over the pellucid waters that held him like a delicate white jewel, Abercrombie admired the tapered hulls, powerful as the sharks over which they sometimes passed. He loved how the sail filled with warm air like an inflated uterus. He loved how the vessel, so elemental and pure, glided over the waves without deforming them. Abercrombie navigated by sight from one ringed island to another in those crumbs of land called Micronesia, from Guam to Bikini, Jaluit to Tarawa, Pukapuka to Manihiki. The coral atolls fascinated him; he spent hours diving down to gaze more closely at this rapturous world nourished by sun and water.

Each island of significant dimensions, he began to notice, was crowned by a small cloud during the day. Yet another triumph: All land carries its mirror image into the sky, its own ghost of white vapor. He was sailing from cloud to cloud. Sometimes the islands he visited were inhabited only by crabs and lacked sources of fresh water. If such was the case, he departed immediately. To slake his thirst, he distilled sea water in the sun, using a condensation device of his own invention. Sometimes he landed on islands where two or perhaps three families lived, either temporarily or permanently; many had never before set eyes on a white man. Abercrombie offered them some provisions or some string, which his hosts accepted with the respect due something so useful. They shared their meals with him. Sometimes a woman came to him in the evening. He never turned her away. In the morning he asked if he might photograph her.

Only once did Abercrombie experience something terrible. It occurred one evening when he had taken a young woman down to the beach. Perhaps she was the daughter of someone whose own people had been banished. In any case he and the young girl were set upon by a howling mob. The young woman ran off with amazing speed under the moon, but a rock from a slingshot struck her in her Achilles tendon and she fell like a wounded horse and got up limping. The crowd had surrounded her in an instant and reduced her to a shredded mass of flesh with their rocks. Abercrombie initially thought that he would die next, but realized that, having himself become taboo, he was untouchable. The mob dispersed into the night without a sound. He forced himself to approach the girl's body and to look at the mass of blood and smashed bone under the blue light of the evening sky. At daybreak he was chased from the island by men carrying long sticks. They ventured near him with their backs turned, so as not to look at him, while the women sang. He reached his catamaran, the red-and-white crabs scattering under his feet.

While those peoples called savages lived out their lives, while the West was tightening its grip upon the world, Richard Abercrombie would finish his world tour, without unseemly haste, humbly, and with the feeling of being both the first and last of his kind. He believed himself immortal. Now, in his grand solitude, everywhere he went was home. He headed slowly back toward what had been his native land and was to be his journey's end.

When Virginie wasn't there to tell him about Abercrombie and Pacific atolls, Kumo grew bored. One day in early October, sitting in his chair, alone in his library, he had to fight an impulse to talk to Virginie's empty chair. She was gone more often now, off working on the biography, or in England for a job interview, or attending a conference of some type. He breathed in deeply, in the hope that a few molecules of her perfume might still be floating in the ambient air. However, the cleaning lady had been there and only the warm remnants of the vacuum cleaner floated in the purified atmosphere. He equally resisted the urge to call Virginie in London. With nothing else to think about, he found his thoughts turning to his past. The previous evening he had received an envelope from Japan but not yet opened it. Again, Hiroshima floated up into his memory, first shrouded in fog and then with greater clarity. Kumo started to remember. He could see the Observatory, the straight lines of the avenues. He tried to think of something else but couldn't.

So Kumo raised himself up and turned toward the sky over Paris. The clouds were so simple and yet strange. It would take men a great deal of time, he thought as he looked at these cottonlike exhalations moving toward the east, to admit that clouds, like all things that occupy time and space, might carry a certain weight. Luke Howard had thought it critical that these diaphanous puffs, these sheets of muslin, these trains of gauze, be perceived as having *mass*. Hence he imagined that water was suspended in the sky, enveloping air in its drops, which were like tiny sacks that he called "vesicles." From the north-facing bay windows, Kumo saw an enormous *cumulo-nimbus* cloud approaching, its base hovering about two thousand feet above the ground. Given that it rose up perhaps three thousand feet—he couldn't see the top of the cloud—it probably weighed a hundred thousand tons. Though Kumo had long gotten used to the idea of cloud weight he also couldn't quite believe in it. His thoughts drifted back to his native city. He remembered the envelope and wondered where he had put it. A hundred thousand tons. The American manatee could weigh a ton. The *cumulo-nimbus* cloud that now had taken over the entire horizon represented the equivalent of a hundred thousand manatees, floating overhead. Again Kumo's thoughts were pushed back down to earth, as if by the huge mass darkening the sky. He thought again of the envelope, which he now remembered he had put in the second drawer of a dresser. He rang a bell and asked that it be brought to him, and also asked that he not be disturbed until the evening nurse arrived. Once delivered into his hands, the envelope, he noted, was actually quite thick. It was from the archives of the Foreign Office in Tokyo, though from the same bureaucrat who had replied to his earlier request, and who was now pleased, as he explained in his cover letter, to be sending other documents relating to Akira Kumo-san's family. There was a booklet made of yellowing paper, like a small family album except that it was covered with official-looking stamps. It had been retrieved from among the ruins of the Japanese embassy in Berlin, following the bomb attack that had killed his parents. The booklet was divided into two parts. At the top was a photograph of Akira at the age of seven, smiling with that self-possession children of that age often exhibit. Kumo barely glanced at it, for his attention was seized by a pair of eyes staring at him from the bottom of the page, great serious-looking eyes set in a moonlike face. He couldn't keep himself from falling into their gaze. They brought everything back—he remembered the name of the little girl, the games they played together, their love for each other, their delight that their parents were someplace in Europe. As he looked into these eyes Akira Kumo's world began to fold in upon him. He started to weep, uncontrollably, and he kept weeping until his eyes had exhausted themselves. When the night nurse arrived, he expressed concern over the redness of Monsieur Kumo's eyes. Kumo assured him it was due to pollution; the weather had been so hot and dry lately, you see, plus there was a slight amount of sulfur in the air.

The next day, a Sunday, Kumo took up one of his felt-tipped pens and began to compose the second part of the letter he had promised Virginie he would write. He had to do it before the memories slipped away again. The day drifted past. In the evening, he gave the letter to the night nurse to mail. After the man had left with it, Kumo locked the door. His wheelchair just managed to squeeze through the passage leading from his office to the main part of his library. Undoing the restraints was the easy part. The next stage was more painful. With his arms, he dragged himself out onto the balcony and up the railing. He was furious that he had to die in order not to live all curled up like a larva. He wasn't killing himself for a particular reason, or to demonstrate anything, but simply because he had no other choice. The only living option—being a decrepit and tedious old man—was of no interest to him. He looked down, to make sure he wouldn't hit anyone. He would yell except that he feared some passerby might run and get an old blanket to catch him, as in some scene from the movies. You never knew. And a third attempt would exceed his abilities. There were some lovely cloud trails with very pretty pink highlights. Tomorrow the weather would be fine, without any doubt, at least in the morning. Kumo knew that he didn't have much time. The night nurse would come back presently. The nurse gave off the faintly acidic odor of sweat, which made Kumo grind his teeth whenever the man adjusted the sheets of his bed; he would prefer never to be near him again. Kumo thought one last time of Virginie and pushed off, believing that his soul would ascend into the empty sky. The impact killed him instantly. Pooling on the sidewalk, his blood created an irregular and rather beautiful design, though it was impossible to tell what it signified.

On November 7, Virginie, who was in London, found a letter waiting for her when she went by Willow Street. For a number of weeks now she had been renting a small apartment in Hampstead. It was noisy, and of course outrageously expensive. She had left Richard Abercrombie after a most unexpected event, which was his announcement to her that he was in love with someone else. The object of his now-monogamous attention was a pretty red-haired woman who taught German literature at the University of London; she had translated into English the works of a contemporary philosopher whose name was lost on Virginie. Like many whose job it is to be intelligent, Nicole Strauss could also be astonishingly naïve about certain matters. From the questions Nicole asked her, Virginie realized—rather quickly, luckily—that Richard had made her out to be his best friend, and that he had led Nicole to believe that Virginie was a militant lesbian. Nicole adored Virginie, but staying there was no longer an option, and she had been happy to move out. She opened the letter and began to read.

The story began when Kumo was thirteen. It was summer, and the weather more beautiful than anyone could remember. Lying in bed, Akira opened his eyes. His sister, Kinoko, was looking at him, laughing. She was always up before him and already dressed in her school uniform. Though a year younger than he, Kinoko was in his class. In Japan it was not customary for a sister to be in the same class as her brother, but the war had changed things; teachers were scarce. Nor was it customary for a brother to feel such love for his younger sister. Their mother, who doted upon their father, had left them to be raised by servants. During the war their parents had been in Europe and rarely came home.

Akira knew that it was time to leave for school, which was a twenty-minute walk along a small path along the bank of the Ota River. They were in summer school, learning how to handle the brushes they would use when they took real courses in calligraphy after the war had ended. If the war ever ended. On their backs they carried lightweight wood frames, onto which were attached, with string, a small water-proof tin box containing their lunch and a polished metal cylinder with their paper and brushes.

It was early August; the war seemed far away. The school's principal, who was also their teacher, punished Akira and Kinoko regularly, for they were not model students. Their schoolmates regarded them with suspicion, but also with envy. They were the ones who organized all the pranks and the games, as well as more innocent activities, such as treasure hunting and hopscotch—for which Akira did amazing drawings and Kinoko devised complicated rules that she changed with exasperating regularity. Sometimes they were so happy they could barely stand to look at each other. They especially loved the walk to school along the meandering river path that went almost the whole distance from their house to the schoolhouse, joining up with the major road only a few hundred feet from their destination. They always had the path to themselves. Only after they had reached the main road did they have to join in the masquerade of communal life. On this morning in August, Kinoko had woken her brother earlier than usual, and Akira knew why—it was so that they could go for a swim first. They would have to dry off before they got to school, and also keep an eye out for the principal, who sometimes took the upper road, where it was less dusty. Of one mind, the children sprinted along the path, which was bordered by sweet-scented bushes, to their favorite spot, a small creek that fed the Ota and at a certain point opened up like a shell. During the night rain had smoothed the black sand on the banks. The air was still; the Ota seemed motionless. The sun shone.

They put their things under a large camphor tree and swam naked, so that they would be dry when they got to school. Besides, it was more fun. It was twenty minutes past seven; class didn't start until 8:30. Again and again they dove down into the pool of clear water, over and over, tirelessly. One dive took so little time that there was always time for another. And that is how all the children of the world, those lucky enough to go at all, get to school late. Suddenly it was ten minutes past eight. Kinoko and Akira would have to hurry. Kinoko climbed onto the sandy bank, which was already warm. She ran to the camphor tree to get dressed. Akira dove one last time. Kinoko raised her head. The sun was hitting the hill behind her. The path wound around a few feet above the creek. Higher up was the paved main road. Akira surfaced ten feet from the edge and turned toward his sister, and while Kinoko was bending down to put on her other sock, a sadly too-familiar silhouette appeared on the road: baggy black suit, white blouse and beige tie, attaché case clutched tight in her right hand, the glint of her large English bracelet-watch, of which she was very proud. No question: It was the principal. She didn't see them at first, for she was walking rigidly straight ahead. It was thirteen minutes past eight. Now Kinoko saw the principal, and because she moved the principal spotted them, raising a menacing finger in their direction. Kinoko responded with a gesture of modesty that distance rendered even more pathetic—she covered herself with a shoe. Akira had an even sillier reaction: he dove down again. It must have been fourteen minutes past eight. He knew he could stay at the bottom for a few moments by taking hold of rocks whose sharp edges were softened by algae. The water was cold. Maybe the principal hadn't recognized them. He knew she wouldn't stoop to coming to the water's edge. Maybe he could deny that he'd been there. The ridiculousness of it all made him laugh, which made him blow out air. He would have to come up.

At that precise moment an unearthly flash of blue light illuminated the creek bed, stunning Akira. Very suddenly he was drowning. A deafening groan, one that seemed to have surged up from the depths of the earth itself, shook the water's surface. Akira rose and made his way to the bank, confused, gasping. At first he didn't notice that Kinoko wasn't there, for everything had changed. Somehow it had become a different day, a different time, a different place. It was much hotter than before, but it was a different kind of heat, as if someone had lit a greasy oven. The ground was gray. A horrible odor floated in the air, the smell of roasted flesh, acidic and fatty at the same time. Even the sky seemed strange.

Akira turned in the direction of the camphor tree. It was gone. Kinoko was gone, too. He started to climb the path, which was covered in burning ash, toward the road. When he reached it he started to run. The principal would tell him what had happened. At the spot where she had been standing lay a red-and-white rag. He leaned over to pick it up and discovered that it was heavy. He recoiled in horrified recognition: It contained the principal's torso. Her legs had been incinerated because they had not been covered in light cloth. He thought about the significance of the camphor tree's disappearance. He didn't yet grasp that Kinoko was dead; there were no remains to make him think that. Kinoko was simply no more, and the lack of evidence was both a relief and nightmarish, because it meant that her body had vanished into the air and that her spirit would wander the earth like a ghost until the end of time. He went back down to the creek, and there he heard the silence—all the birds within a radius of five miles were dead, and so were most of the people, and the insects, too. On the troubled surface of the Ota River floated the white bodies of fish. Where the camphor tree had been he found a half-melted metal object. It was Kinoko's small German pocket watch. It was too hot to pick up. He gathered some water from the creek in his hands and splashed it over the watch. The crystal was gone and the hands had been fused into the face at 8:15. Akira threw it into the cinders.

He started to walk toward the city along the road, strewn with scraps of things he couldn't identify. He came across several people who were dying, many more who were already dead, and some body parts, until he came to the place where the school had stood. He continued to walk, though his feet were blistered. He walked in order to walk. No one could have told him that going toward a place so pulverised and toxic was a mistake. No one yet knew. He arrived at the city gates. A woman covered in glass shards was somehow managing to stumble along. The gates sat on a small hill where the children had once liked to sit, the two of them, and from here Akira looked out upon a plain of desolation like nothing he had seen before. It wasn't like those bombed German cities, photos of which he had seen in the newspaper. This was more ruined than that, the destruction was more complete and more uniform.

The holy book the Americans worshipped foretold the end of the world, a tale of blood and fire in which the wicked were punished. Over the city was hanging a single gigantic cloud straight out of that story, come to earth. It was as if the flattened city, reduced to nothing, was floating above itself, as if this cloud had absorbed all the ash the city had exhaled— the dust of roads and buildings, and bodies as well. At the other end of the earth, in northeast Europe, Jews and gypsies and political prisoners and others had also disappeared into ash, and had been for years, but the world had looked elsewhere. (Eventually they built monuments to them, monuments that would, perversely, only serve to help us to forget.) The Hiroshima cloud was of a very particular kind that no one, aside from a few on a military base in New Mexico, had seen before. It was a tall cloud, anchored to the ground by an enormously long stalk: a cloud on a pedestal, like a grotesque mushroom. Akira sat on the small hill and watched. Slowly the gargantuan thing started to lose its mooring and to move, like a dirigible without a pilot. Then it turned black, a black deep as night, until it gradually choked off the entire horizon, plunging Hiroshima into darkness, though if you looked behind you, away from the city, you could see the sun was still shining. The cloud expanded, expanded to the point of breaking. It started to rain. The rain was black, blackening the dust and ash. It would rain like this every evening for weeks. Looking at the inklike droplets, Akira tried not to think about his sister. Two hours before these drops, she had been a young girl and now her body fell as rain, and this had become a world in which such a thing—and many other things besides—was conceivable. Akira started to cry. Toward evening an emergency team found the young boy, naked, without visible wounds, sitting on a hill overlooking Hiroshima. They took him with them. They couldn't simply allow him to stay there all night.

Akira exhibited no symptoms of cancer; he didn't suffer even the slightest infection connected with having been at Hiroshima on August 6, 1945. Akira told the Americans nothing. He let them run their tests but remained silent—about his sister, and about being underwater when the bomb went off (which in any case would not be enough to explain his immunity). For weeks he lived surrounded by people dying, people of all ages, more of them every day. When he ran away to Tokyo he was thirteen years old. He believed himself immortal. He was drawing and sketching constantly; he was nearly crazy; no one noticed this. You have to be crazy to forget Hiroshima, yet forgetting was the only way to survive. So he did.

Kumo's letter ended as abruptly as it had begun. Virginie got on the first available flight to Paris. She knew there was no hope. His body had been laid out in the library on Rue

Lamarck; they had repaired the head as best they could. Virginie did not ask to go straight up. She entered through the glass doors of the main entry. Journalists were milling around, shouting questions at anyone going in or coming out. The custodial staff, the models and designers—everyone was in tears. Men in dark suits barked orders into slender gray cell phones, trying to keep it together. The boardroom was to the left of the main entry. Sitting around an enormous black lacquer table were lawyers, businessmen, fashion people. A small, serious-looking man at the head of the table signaled to Virginie to come forward and sit next to him, and then he began proceedings.

Akira Kumo, it would seem, liked to make wills. About twenty of them had been found stuffed into an unlocked trunk. The serious-looking man was about to read out loud the most recent of them. The others were sealed. Akira Kumo declared that he was of sound mind and body and without heirs, direct or indirect. The fashion house should and must be preserved. The deceased authorized it to expand operations into a line of luxury accessories intended specifically for the general market, the sort of mass production that until now he had refused to allow. There was a clause involving the Foundation. Finally there was a clause pertaining to Virginie Latour. She was to be given the ashes of the deceased, to dispose of in any way she saw fit, but she should not do so in the presence of any other person or reveal their location to anyone. There was to be no ceremony, whether secular or religious, public or private, to honor his memory. No one was to attend the cremation. An envelope contained the keys to a house in London that the deceased wished to bequeath to his librarian. His work finished, the serious-looking man rose to his feet, and everyone else followed suit. They left through an inner court.

Virginie was taken up to the library—she felt she couldn't refuse now—to view the body. She was left alone with it. She walked over to the bay window, just as she had done so many times before, and then went through the glass doors and out onto the small balcony. At the end of Rue Lamarck sat a massive cloud. Rather than look at the body she would look at this cloud, squatting at the end of Rue Lamarck, and at the indifferent sky. She assumed that Kumo's body had already lost its water content, and that by now that water had become condensation on the inside of the window. Soon they would air the room out. The moisture would remain for a while, and then be evaporated by the sun. Some portion of it would reach the pavement below, running along the drains and into the gutters and sewers until it reached the Seine, and after that the sea, leaving behind no trace. Virginie pointed herself in the direction of the cloud, the direction of the sea and of the rising sun. Then she left the *hôtel particulier* on Rue Lamarck.

Kumo's staff gave Virginie a complete file on her new place of employ. Her former patron had done as he promised. The European Centre for Medium-Range Weather Forecasts in Reading, a half-hour's train ride west of London, had been looking for a part-time archivist. Virginie called and inquired, and found out as much as she could about her new job. Her ability in English seemed to reassure the Centre's director. Then she went to look at the house Kumo had left her. The address was 6 Well Walk, a two-story brick house with a flat roof in Hampstead. It was entirely white except for the upper windows, which were pale blue. A plaque on the front wall informed passersby that a poet had lived there for a number of years, at a time before Hampstead had been absorbed by London. It was steps from the Heath. When she walked into the sitting room with its pine floor, Virginie knew immediately that this was where she would live. Sitting on the only table in the room was a gray porphyry vase. Finally she was able to weep.

The next day she went to Reading. Financed by the European Council, the Centre is one of the finest in the world, equipped to process calculations from all of Western Europe's weather forecasters. The job would require Virginie to spend three days a week in Reading, cataloguing the books and meteorological journals that arrived regularly, and helping to promote the image of the Centre and its work. On Thursdays and Fridays, Virginie would stay home and spend the morning working on the Abercrombie biography; in the afternoons she turned to the *Protocol,* going over the layouts of the proofs as well as different versions of the images being reproduced. On Saturdays she often had dinner with Nicole Strauss, who was becoming a friend, and sometimes with Nicole and Richard both. The rest of the time she enjoyed being at home, or went for walks on the Heath, or visited a museum. When she wrote she pretended she was talking to Kumo; this gave her courage. After she had lived in the house for six months she hired a contractor to install a skylight over her bed.

The weeks passed like days. In January Virginie reached the three-quarter point in the *Protocol.* Abercrombie's notes were becoming terser, but she was becoming increasingly adept at following their meaning. Having reached the end of the world, the end of all races and women and places, Abercrombie might still have continued his journey, but he was tired. He needed, he decided, to go back to his native land, to take the full measure of his transformation. By telegram he sent instructions that his mail be forwarded to San Francisco. He would now begin to move in the direction of England, though at a deliberate pace and by means of a route that would enable him to complete the world tour. In October 1892 Abercrombie was in Hawaii and by December had reached San Francisco Bay. Fog prevented him from seeing anything of the city at first, but he found the cloud enveloping it completely delightful. He spent an hour on the upper deck of the ship staring into it while waiting for the tide that would permit him to go ashore.

A fresh bundle of mail awaited him at the front desk of the Grand Hotel. It had been a year since he had made contact with anyone. He couldn't comprehend why his absence seemed to have created such furor among the scientific community, apparently caused by his deliberate silence on the subject of his photographic cloud atlas—a silence interpreted by those who knew him as a sure sign that it would prove a triumph. Richard Abercrombie, they said, was maintaining his silence in order to make his eventual victory all the more stunning. He didn't bother opening the important-looking mail, to the astonishment of the receptionist who had lent him his letter opener and who was staring curiously at this white man, whose skin tone and dress suggested those of a sailor and yet who was the recipient of such impressive correspondence. The letter from his banker in London was the only one Abercrombie opened. The tone was admonitory. Bankers become upset when their clients waste money. As directed, Abercrombie went to the local branch of the bank associated with his own, and there he learned from the mouth of a slight little man with a pale face—a little man in a well-cut suit who had perhaps never in his life tasted a woman, and with a civilized mouth from which emanated the

smell of gin and tobacco, and which undertook this unpleasant message with painful embarrassment—that the funds of
Professor Abercrombie had in recent months been quite
seriously eroded, and while it was not irreversible, Farmer,
Johnson, & Farmer Sons, Ltd., respectfully wished to inform
their client that, should he choose (and naturally this would
be well within his rights) to pursue this course, it became the
solemn duty of M. M. Farmer, acting on behalf of F, J&F,
Ltd., to inform him that such a pace of expenditure ran very
grave risks indeed were it to continue in the months and perhaps even years ahead at this rate, and thus that they had no
option but to envision that in less than five years, should prevailing economic conditions neither improve nor decline,
there would be a reduction in income commensurate with
said expenditures. Once Abercrombie had managed to extract from the bank employee that he was not ruined but
rather simply being offered the advice of a prudent banker,
he left, though not before wiring M. M. Farmer and their associate Johnson, demanding that they send him a large sum
of money, and if necessary sell a number of bonds to accomplish this, without the slightest delay. He gave no address. He
would come to collect the funds in person.

Abercrombie returned to the Grand Hotel and asked for
the bill. He offered no forwarding address for his mail. A
large tip assured that the receptionist would destroy any further letters that arrived addressed to him. Carrying his own
luggage, a single trunk that dug into his shoulder, Abercrombie made his way to a hotel located at the edge of Chinatown.
From his first-floor room he looked out into the street
through muslin curtains that might once have been white.

The man in the striped suit was still there. From the moment Abercrombie had arrived in San Francisco he had been followed by this man, whom he had seen talking to sailors from his ship. He seemed quite young, and had been so cautious in his surveillance movements that everyone in the port had taken note of him. He wore a monocle, perhaps in order to appear older than he was. He also seemed to be in pain. Abercrombie felt that everyone he came across seemed sickly and pale; he was beginning to realize this was typical of all Western city dwellers, all the office workers and merchants and factory workers and housemaids. He left the hotel, the young man following him from a distance. He ducked into the first alley he came to and hid behind some crates. After the young man passed by, Abercrombie caught up with him and put a hand on his shoulder. The young man stopped, frozen, having understood immediately what had happened. He turned, his face flushing violet, making him seem even younger than before. Abercrombie smiled.

James Paul James Gardiner, Jr., was the San Francisco correspondent for the Washington-based *Weather Bureau.* He offered Abercrombie a few lame excuses for his behavior, trying to explain rather than deny his actions. He wondered whether they might go off for some refreshment. Abercrombie, who was thirsty, agreed and suggested they try out an establishment on the corner called the Chinese Dragon. They descended some badly stained wooden steps and entered a high-ceilinged room where a handful of old men were playing mah-jong. Like many timid individuals fearful of silence, Gardiner talked continuously, making large, rapid gestures with his hands. They sat down. Two pints of beer arrived.

Gardiner continued to babble. He hadn't dared to present himself to the professor, whose career he had been following practically since childhood. He had kept up with recent developments and in fact had read an issue of the *Indonesian Chronicle* containing a fascinating article about that confrontation with the ferocious orangutan. He should have simply introduced himself, he knew that now. Yet he hadn't felt he could permit himself that kind of liberty and was more comfortable watching the professor from a distance. On it went. Gardiner wasn't such a bad fellow. Abercrombie, who hadn't consumed any alcohol in over a year, was drunk even before he'd finished his pint. He smiled benevolently at his voluble young admirer, without taking in a third of what he was nattering on about. This seemed not to deter Gardiner, who pronounced himself deeply honored to have met so distinguished a figure as Professor Abercrombie. He talked about science and progress, and had lots of questions to ask the author of *Principles of Meteorological Forecasting*. In fact he himself had jotted down a number of observations regarding the morning mists in Napa Valley right here in California, and he would be most pleased and humbled to show them to Professor Abercrombie. Finally, Gardiner, reddening once again, dared to inquire as to the progress of the photographic project that had been announced to the scientific community in Paris. It was Abercrombie's turn to become flushed. No one would ever see his journal. The other clients in the Chinese Dragon—opium smokers, down-at-the-heels sailors—had initially stared suspiciously at these two thin and talkative men, but now paid them no attention. Abercrombie was by this point quite drunk and decided to enjoy himself. He ordered another round. To rid himself as gracefully as possible of Gardiner—half to make the young man happy and half for his own amusement—Abercrombie started talking in very serious tones about everything and nothing in particular. He would, he said, be able to show a considerable number of images, without elaborating on what these images would be of. First he needed to find a way of presenting them. They would require accompaniment by a written text, one explaining to the world what he had seen and documented. In a hushed voiced and with an ecstatic expression, not quite believing his own audacity, Gardiner wondered whether Professor Abercrombie might not call such a text and the images that went with it a...*protocol*. With that air of mysterious profundity characteristic of the inebriated, Abercrombie replied conspiratorially that indeed, this was exactly what it was: a *protocol*.

Thirty years later, for a special issue of the *Weather Bureau Monthly* devoted to the pioneers of modern meteorology, James Paul James Gardiner, Jr., the well-known specialist in crop irrigation, would recall the events of that day. For three decades he had cherished its memory, holding on determinedly to the smallest detail so that it wouldn't grow hazy. Naturally, this meant that for thirty years he had also been embellishing the story, which became a principle source of the *Protocol*'s legendary status. For his part, Abercrombie would always remember the expression of rapture on the face of this slight young man, whose path he would never again cross. Not long before his own death, he wrote THE ABERCROMBIE PROTOCOL in violet ink across the green cover of his notebook.

Gardiner had begged Professor Abercrombie to let him accompany him back to his hotel, but the meteorologist had refused the offer. Perhaps tomorrow morning he could drop off a copy of his notes regarding the morning mists in Napa Valley? Naturally he could, came the reply. As soon as he was alone, Abercrombie hoisted his trunk onto his shoulder and

changed hotels. He took the first street he came to in Chinatown and soon found an opium den where women were available. No one would think to look for him there. He rented a
room for two weeks and paid in advance. He had decided
to extend his research to include all the world's regions.
Intuition was telling him that the sexual inclinations of the
various human races were a function of climate. Science de-
manded that he put this hypothesis to the test. San Francisco
was the center of the emergent world: Halfway between Europe and Asia, it offered the perfect setting for this kind of
study. Abercrombie stayed on there for three months, during which he slept with the natives of as many nations as he
could. The rest of the time he walked the city he had fallen
in love with because of its resemblances to his own destiny.
San Francisco maintained no attachment to its past; it was
populated but lacked a population; and it was a place where
each might live as he pleased. An unconquerable repugnance
kept Abercrombie from physical contact with women from
his own country, even with women from continental Europe.
Very soon—in a period during which the scientific community lost all trace of him, and during which poor Gardiner,
meanwhile, was wildly anxious, trying to persuade the city's
police force that Professor Abercrombie had been the victim
of kidnapping—Abercrombie became a fixture in San Francisco's red-light district. He was the one to whom one brought
non-Western women, so long as their nationality didn't appear on the list he had given the bordello's manager, a list that
kept growing.

The owner of the opium-den-cum-bordello where Abercrombie had chosen to take up residence sold him a strange

religious text. Taoist in origin, it had been edited by an eccentric British scholar; it was lavishly illustrated and completely pornographic. Turning one of the pages, Abercrombie came upon the image of a small naked boy, laughing, his left hand holding his penis, a finger stuck in the corner of his mouth. In other lithographs he was pictured beneath a woman or women. Abercrombie became curious about this spying little imp. He learned that the boy's name was T'un Y'un, and that he was a minor figure in Taoist mythology—the greatest mischief maker among the lesser divinities in the Chinese pantheon. Legend had it that in addition to being a prankster, T'un Y'un was also the most dissolute of the gods. When the Earth was formed he hadn't been given a serious job, such as guiding a star; instead, he was assigned the task of shepherding herds of clouds. It was T'un Y'un who orchestrated the playful movements of sky and water, and he governed the principles of flow and moisture. Abercrombie believed that he had found his god.

He crossed the United States from west to east, but without taking much in. For centuries the world had sent its unwanted here. No nation was more diverse than this one, and yet all the inhabitants shared primitive manners and that casual indifference that is the hallmark of the West. Abercrombie was unaffected, however; his highly evolved spirituality helped him ignore appearances and to see in each thing a unique combination—an utterly unique combination—of simple elements that was at the same time connected to the profound unity of all living matter. A large quantity of water, a variety of minerals, a complex chemistry, a gentle electrical force: These, to him, represented a human being, living in the confines of the Earth and yet, since the beginning of the modern era, seeking to estrange himself from it. Abercrombie crossed the United States, and everywhere he went he confronted those alien dreams called cities. He passed through Salt Lake City, where the Mormons had thought themselves blessed when they came across a dead sea spreading out before them. He passed through Cincinnati, where impoverished Germans had believed they had returned to the Ruhr Valley. He went to a bordello in Chicago, but found the women's flesh too sad.

In Washington, in September 1893, Abercrombie was first stricken with the symptoms of the disease that would eventually kill him; until then he had enjoyed perfect health. It started with a cough and flulike symptoms. After that he got a skin infection, and then a second, followed by digestive troubles and a host of other ailments. When he realized how serious it was, he stayed in bed, permitting himself to be seen by as few people as possible, living quietly to avoid dying too quickly. Encumbering as they were, these symptoms become of deep interest to him. His body became the central focus of his thought. He had started to believe that nothing happened by chance. The onslaught of this protean disease was tangible evidence of his genius. He had no doubt that his body was being colonized by these exterior life-forms because he had experienced carnality with more races than anyone else in the world. A disease was a life-form like any other. This one threatened the life of the individual known as Richard Abercrombie—true enough—but it also proved that his theories were correct.

Sometimes Abercrombie felt as if he were the first of a whole new species, and sometimes the last. He was not afraid of death; he had distributed his semen throughout the world and the elements that briefly merged to produce it would surely pursue their own lives among the incessant metamorphosis that is the living universe. He sensed the advent of a new Middle Ages, a time of invasion and crusade, of the intermingling of cultures and races, a period of extraordinary inventions. That this ineluctable evolution might also involve the spread of a deadly disease did not surprise him. The Middle Ages had suffered through the Black Death. By early spring 1894, when the first warm days came to Washington, Abercrombie decided to cross the Atlantic. His health was deteriorating, and he believed that a more temperate climate would retard the end.

The line of the horizon was discolored by a trail of stringy, indistinct, and fast-moving clouds. It was the coast of England. The boat passed Southampton and continued to Gravesend. Abercrombie took passage on a barge that moved with painful slowness up the Thames, which smelled of iodinated mud and damp coal. London seemed darker and infinitely older than he remembered and he by contrast felt younger without his moustache and his long hair pulled back and tied at the base of his neck, like a sailor in former days. He still refused to sleep with English women.

He had also decided to keep his distance from the scientific community; appreciation of his genius would be posthumous. His green notebook had swelled to an enormous size, containing, in all, two thousand photographs of women. On the way to London, Abercrombie reflected upon how to conclude his opus. The idea of an essay devoted to infinity had been going through his head since he'd been crossing the South Pacific toward California and watched the endless flow of the wake as the boat ploughed the waves.

He had been in London for two weeks when he knew it was time to face the inevitable and make contact with his family. He had put it off as long as he could. To accustom himself to the idea he decided to move back into his house. Because of course Richard Abercrombie had a house in London, though he had not even considered going there after his arrival, having grown so used to living in hotels. It was a large townhouse located in Kensington. He rang the bell. The door was opened by the butler, the son and grandson and great-grandson of someone who had worked for the family. The man didn't flinch when he saw who was there, but calmly stood aside, pronouncing his pleasure at seeing Professor Abercrombie again and politely requesting to be informed what Professor Abercrombie would be requiring in terms of staff to meet his needs. Abercrombie replied that the ridiculously low number of five would be sufficient. The Abercrombie clan hosted two gatherings twice a month during the height of the social season. Richard was added to the guest list of the next function, making it clear his relatives gave no credence to the rumors regarding either his disappearance or his mental condition. He made it known that he would attend the one being held two days hence.

The afternoon luncheon was deemed a great success, costing the Abercrombies fifty times what a miner in north Cardiff would make in a year—his labors being one of the chief sources of the family's wealth, though one would not have guessed this from the impeccable lawns and bleached tablecloths. The ladies amused themselves with archery. At the end of one alley of trees Abercrombie felt a sudden jolt of emotion, recognizing one of his favorite childhood dogs. The animal did not recognize him, however, and growled at his approach, which was when Abercrombie realized that of course the animal was probably the great-great-grandson of the dog he knew. Beneath one of the canopies erected for the occasion sat his mother, surrounded as ever by a small crowd of men. Though her husband had been dead for twenty years, she continued to wear black, in part because she looked so stunning in it. Abercrombie remembered how he had adored her as a child.

A formidable-looking group of gentlemen approached and encircled him—his cousins and his younger brother, John. The Abercrombies had never proven unworthy of the respect and gratitude of the Crown; their number included a bishop and several close advisers to Her Majesty. They spoke to Richard with an enthusiasm all the more sincere once they had taken stock of the fact that he was not, in fact, deranged. His brother took him aside. The nature of their conversation was not a little difficult to follow, but it slowly emerged from the diplomatic patter that John Abercrombie hoped to ascertain what his elder brother's intentions were. Richard was breathtakingly direct in his reply. He informed John that he did not intend to represent in an official capacity the Abercrombie name; nor would he return to the family's properties in Scotland. He would live in retirement in London. His brother ran to give their mother the happy news. Richard returned to Kensington.

A recluse, he continued to work on the essay that would conclude the *Protocol.* The enormous number of natural forms seemed irregular: The straight line, the circle, and the cube

were rarely to be found on this planet. The side of a mountain, a vaginal wall, the surface of a grain of wheat—all featured irregularities of varying degrees of significance. But
Western science had never truly taken account of the sinuos-
ity, the anfractuosities that one discovers through careful study
of these things. A geometrician asked to measure the length
of the coastline of England would calculate its irregularities
as so many tiny segments of straight lines connected end to
end. Such approximation might be practical, but it was deceptive. Were one to go to the trouble of measuring out the
coastal twists and turns, they would prove quite long because
they are in fact not straight. It would take years to walk Cornwall's coast, particularly if whoever undertook such a task followed every deviation and contour, and even then the final
measurements would not be perfect. The tiniest irregularity
itself consists of even tinier irregularities, and so on, such
that we would have to conclude that the coastline was infinite. So, too, all objects in nature: the outline of an ear, a child's
hand, a woman's stomach. These are also infinite. The word
"infinite" was the last word that Richard Abercrombie wrote
in his book. His work was completed.

The disease whittled away at him. During his first year or
two back, he found it entertaining to consult doctors about
his conditions, but eventually lost all respect for these fellow
men of science who grew impatient with the intractability of
their patient's ailment, which was unique. Most avoided him,
wishing to escape censure for being unable to cure the famous Abercrombie. One day, one of these exasperated physi-
cians accused Abercrombie of making his illness up. At that,
Abercrombie closed his door to them all for good. He had

the wood crates containing his medical files nailed shut and taken down to the basement, keeping only a small drawing one doctor had done on the back of an envelope to show a patient what his tuberculosis looked like. You could see from the drawing why Abercrombie had kept it: The tiny air sacks resembled spider egg pouches or miniature *cumulus* clouds filled with blood. Soon the diseases afflicting him began to overwhelm his faculties. He began to wander in his thoughts, sometimes for entire days. He was settled in the front parlor of his house, in an armchair near a bay window, though he looked at neither the sky nor at the street.

Finally he came upon a name for his science: analogy. No other word would do. "Isomorphism" was more precise than "analogy," certainly, but it didn't sound right. To validate this new name, Abercrombie tried it out in a variety of settings. For example, he would say out loud in a booming voice, *Professor Abercrombie has just been named to the Chair of Analogy that has been created for him at Cambridge.* He also tried out a number of titles: *Principles of Applied Analogy; Analogy as Used by Children and People of Sex.* Soon he was daydreaming of an Institute of Analogical Anthropology. He saw himself at the Royal Academy of Medicine, in a vast amphitheater lit by electricity, demonstrating female sexual organs of all races to an audience of doctors, philosophers, and enlightened observers; they would applaud when he explained the natural indolence of Negroes and their innate sensuality, as well as the hypertrophy of their secondary sexual organs. He had completely forgotten about wanting posthumous fame. The servants had to wash the fabric of the chair cover, which smelled of urine and diarrhea, quite often.

In December of 1893, the Meteorological Congress had convened in Vienna, the gathering at which Richard Abercrombie was to have presented his Photographic Atlas. He hadn't attended, pleading his illness, but in a message to the president of the congress he acknowledged the victory of his illustrious colleague William S. Williamsson: the true Universal Cloud Atlas could only contain lithographs done by artists under the supervision of scientists. The photographic image was too unreliable, too falsely objective. Nonetheless, Williamsson's triumph was shortlived: Two days before the end of the congress, his body was discovered in a bordello in the center of town. The fashionable lady who had gone with him to frolic with a streetwalker while Williamsson watched had taken flight the instant he had started to suffocate. By the time the prostitute returned with the madam, he was dead. The madam immediately noted his social rank and went through his pockets, finding his journal in one of them. Her efforts were rewarded when she managed to wring out of the president of the congress a considerable sum in exchange for her silence, and for her arranging to have Williamsson's corpse transported discreetly back to his hotel. Officially, the body of the famous meteorologist was discovered in his room by the Imperial Hotel's house detective. The congress interrupted its program and organized a tribute. Between Abercrombie's absence and Williamsson's death, many veterans felt as if the Vienna congress marked the end of an era.

The *Protocol*'s legend grew. The less often its author appeared in public the greater the speculation about it. As a reminder of old times, a Scottish colleague sent Abercrombie a copy of the closing speech of the Vienna Congress. He read it carefully. Something had changed, and in so short a period of time. Meteorology had come of age. Throughout the West, farmers, generals, and ships' captains waited for the bulletins that would dictate a good portion of their activities. Each morning in London, before the maid arrived to open the curtains, air out the room, and serve breakfast, a lonely old man rose slowly from his bed and bowed slightly before a bronze statue of a chubby, laughing child that had been placed on the veranda. The statue was not top quality, but the dealer on Gerard Street had assured him it was an authentic votive figure from the Song Dynasty, and of a deity called T'un Y'un. He was the lord of the clouds, said the dealer, and floated wherever his fancy took him.

After breakfast, the old man wrapped himself in a quilt and settled in a chair next to T'un Y'un. There was a popular new method of smoking called cigarettes that enchanted him, and he did it under the watchful eye of his god—and to the despair of his valet. One purchased these cigarettes pre-rolled, and they featured a cellulose filter. Abercrombie loved to smoke. On sunny days he would sit on his veranda, opening his mouth and letting the smoke drift out. He watched the rising smoke until it disappeared. Sometimes he let a cigarette burn itself out in the ashtray. Initially the smoke went straight up, and then, as if following some unseen directive, it would begin to writhe like a snake until it disappeared. Sometimes a fly disturbed the plumes as they rose and created erratic refinements.

Richard Abercrombie died in 1917. This was not a particularly good year in which to die. Millions throughout Europe were doing the same thing; the newspapers printed endlessly long lists of their names. When for example the body of a member of the Royal Society was found in a trench, the *Times* would offer a respectful but distracted obituary. In this context Abercrombie himself was deemed worthy of a few paragraphs. He expired rejoicing in the idea that a wild proliferation of living organisms was attached to his dying body. The Abercrombie clan delegated his brother to make arrangements. That was when they learned about Richard's best-kept secret: his eleven-year-old daughter.

The so-called Abigail Abercrombie Affair began at the end of 1912, when Richard Abercrombie stipulated in his will that his *Protocol* was to be published the day following his death. In the summer of 1912, just when the Katmai volcano buried Kodiak Island in the Aleutians under tons of ash, Abercrombie learned that his family would try to get their hands on his *Protocol*. He knew precisely how they would regard his photographs, his sketches of shells and flowers, and his meditations. His will wouldn't protect him. History was filled with inventors, philosophers, and artists betrayed by their families. To safeguard his work, Abercrombie decided upon an insane strategy—he would make a complete stranger his heir. There was considerable commotion in the Abercrombie household on the day when the master of the house announced that he planned to go out. Two hours later an automobile pulled up, and Abercrombie got in it. The small staff observed this novel event from the kitchen window.

The Orphanage for Sons and Daughters of the Navy was a tall, narrow building at the eastern end of Fleet Street. Large society ladies generally visited at Christmastime to pat the children on the heads and to receive flowers. Though the structure's façade was severe looking, those who worked within its walls were quite dedicated. When the automobile pulled up before the main door, the orphanage's director, a tall Anglican nun who looked as dry as an old biscuit, was there to greet this distinguished member of the Royal Academy of Sciences. Some children were paraded before him. Neat and well-groomed, these were the cream of the crop, the ones who had excelled in their schoolwork and been the most assiduous in their religious studies. Abercrombie looked them over politely. Lunch was served in the large, bright refectory. The staff and Abercrombie sat on a raised platform. After lunch the children were permitted to play on the grounds behind the orphanage, grounds that were actually quite beautiful given that they were located in the heart of the City. The solemn and carefully choreographed dance of adoption was performed around the visitor, while the candidates pretended to manners or sophistication far beyond their years. Abercrombie spied a little girl of around six, standing apart from the others. Like them she was neatly dressed and her hair was combed, but she was preoccupied with spitting into a puddle. Despite all the efforts of the staff and to the obvious consternation of the director, she was the one Abercrombie chose. He announced that he wished to take her with him straightaway. A ripple of murmuring went through the staff; the director looked at the other sisters, who were averting their gaze. The year before, a small boy from the orphanage had been legally adopted and his poor unspeakably abused body been found floating in the Thames. Abercrombie's generous donation to the orphanage, that they might continue their good works, only heightened their concerns. In the end, however, the director gave her consent. During the drive to Kensington, little Abigail fell asleep leaning against Abercrombie, who was himself already asleep.

Perhaps it was hereditary, perhaps caused by the deprivations of her early infancy, but the adoptive daughter of Richard Abercrombie turned into a grubby and ungrateful little brat. Worn down by his illnesses, her father seemed unfazed. Her tantrums were a sign of a willful personality; her refusal to learn indicated a precocious independence of spirit. The cook didn't help matters by becoming ridiculously fond of the child, spoiling her beyond all reason.

Time passed. The world didn't grow older and wiser, indeed quite the opposite; the new century revealed a nearly adolescent infatuation with horror and destruction. In 1915, Abercrombie read in the newspapers that the meteorological sciences were destroying themselves with increasing skill. During the war, which was to have been short but which dragged on and on among the plains of northern France, advances in the study of wind were helping with the use of poison gas; advances in the understanding of cloud cover were permitting more effective troop deployments. It was written in the professional journals that these new contraptions called "aero planes" would help patriotic young meteorologists make ever more breathtaking breakthroughs. Abercrombie was by now in steep decline and would spend hours watching drool roll down his chest. So deep ran his bitterness toward the scientific community that he refused to bequeath his papers to the Royal Academy.

One might have hoped that his deathbed would be the scene of noble farewells, or offer an opportunity for him to sum up his life's achievements and their profound interconnectivity, or perhaps involve a final tearful conversation between a father and his adoptive daughter. None of that happened. On the night of December 4, 1917, he was found slumped in his favorite chair. He hadn't called for help or cried out. In his report the attending physician described the cause of death as "general exhaustion," which was both stunningly forthright and an indication of his lack of comprehension.

Learning that Abigail would inherit everything, the family decided to contain the scandal by not registering an official challenge. The cook—who, remarkably, was not a greedy person—was offered a fair salary and appointed the girl's tutor. They were left on their own in the handsome townhouse, which was showing signs of wear. So were Abercrombie's personal assets. Yet the remnants of a nineteenth-century fortune were substantial enough to live comfortably in the twentieth. The caretakers of Abercrombie's finances did their work well. By the time she reached her majority, Abigail was a wealthy young woman.

She did not change with the years, and her precocious indulgence in all the vices never flagged. Once she had become rich, she devoted several years to throwing her little fortune out the window of several hotels along the French coast, or into the pockets of various men of handsome mien who had neither professions nor discernible sources of income. Back in London, she became the center of her crew of debauched companions who inhabited small hovels on the banks of the Thames, where she shacked up with sailors and unemployed dockworkers who sometimes beat her. At thirty-five she looked fifty. An unrepentant drunk, she was, nonetheless, not an idiot. Having been forced to decode the flowery letters of men of science from around the world, she realized the value of her adoptive father's papers, including a trunk that was filled with travel letters, unpublished articles, and memoirs. Her assessment of their worth was confirmed when she placed an advertisement in the *Times,* announcing that she was seeking the help of an expert to catalogue these papers, and received in reply some thirty responses from potential candidates. Thus it was in 1941 that a small, round, bearded Latvian named Anton Vries presented himself at the house in Kensington. Abigail made her conditions clear. Professor Vries would do a complete inventory of the papers at no cost to her, and in exchange would be permitted to publish them with whatever commentary he wished to add. By chance on the evening before his arrival she had stumbled upon a large notebook stuffed with photographic proofs and filled with handwritten notes. Opening it at random she found herself staring at a woman's sex, small and nacreous as a seashell. She wasn't in the least taken aback, though she could make no sense of the accompanying text. She knew that she was holding the *Protocol,* about which so many scientists had been haranguing her from the moment she turned eighteen. She said nothing about it to Anton Vries, who completed his inventory within a few days, disappointed not to have gotten his hands on the famous *Protocol*, though also certain that the publication of his *Observations Concerning the Abercrombie Archive* would be enough to earn him a chair of geography. Abigail consulted a lawyer, who drew up a contract that Vries had no choice except to sign. In exchange for authenticating a certain document, an inventory of which he would not be permitted to make public, he would be appointed editor of the Williamsson-Abercrombie correspondence, which Abigail was preparing to auction off. Vries agreed to the terms. The bibliographical description of the *Protocol* he produced, and which Abigail sent to be published in the *Bulletin of World Meteorological Organization*, was a masterpiece of bibliophilic detail and yet deeply deceptive, for it revealed nothing about the notebook's actual contents. Collectors and cloud lovers the world over were incensed.

And so began for Abigail a long juggling act. She would neither deny nor confirm any rumor regarding the *Protocol*, leading one party to understand that its sentimental value was so great that she could not part with it, and another to deduce that it was not suitable for publication. Though no one was taken in by her intentions, the *Protocol*'s fame began to grow. Like many uneducated people Abigail mistrusted banks, and could not bring herself to place it in a safe-deposit box. She spent hours lugging the notebook around the house in Kensington until at last she found a hiding place she deemed satisfactory.

In 1946, at forty years of age, she became pregnant. She had no idea who might be the father. Her pregnancy led her to a new appreciation of her body and the sweet joys of attending to it. She stopped drinking—astonishingly, without the slightest difficulty—and stopped prowling the wharves. She prayed, a little absurdly, that her child might inherit her father's mental faculties. Out of superstition she gave the child her father's name. Richard Abercrombie would always remember his mother as a small, angular woman with dry hands and scrupulous modesty who was always quite severe with him and yet who loved him to distraction. He was a well-behaved child and a model student, then a studious and proper young man. Abigail was deeply disappointed when he abandoned law for psychoanalysis. Still, she kept all his articles in a small cabinet she had specifically designed for the purpose, as well as a beautifully bound copy of his case studies.

After she turned one hundred her decline was rapid. Her son visited her daily at Whittington Hospital, and she told him how certain she was that the dark-skinned doctors and nurses were trying to kill her. The day before her death, Abigail revealed the *Protocol*'s hiding place to her son; along with the house, it was the only thing she had to leave him. She hoped he might sell it but asked that he not read it first, out of respect for his grandfather. He thanked her effusively, promising solemnly that he would not read it. He had known of the *Protocol*'s existence since the age of ten; at twelve, he had discovered its hiding place. He learned how to put it back in its place under two floorboards in the broom closet without making the door creak. For years he masturbated looking at his grandfather's images.

The summer promised to be hot and humid: a summer of clouds. Virginie spent it in London. (Her first vacation days would come at Christmas.) She had everything she needed there. She got to know Hampstead and its Heath, which was located so nearby her little white house. She went there on the days when she didn't need to be in Reading, and always with a spirit of quiet piety for its small valleys and grassy hillsides where the thistles grew. Several centuries had not much altered the Heath, though the nights are no longer black; satellite images show that nowhere in Europe is darkness absolute. Nonetheless Virginie wanted to believe that the place where Luke Howard once went on his walks had not changed. How good it felt to tramp the same paths as the dead, and with the same sensation of pleasure. She walked with veneration among the trees that, during their youth, had seen women wearing crinoline and carrying parasols passing by, holding the arms of handsome young gentlemen.

———

Occasionally during the day Virginie lay on her bed beneath the skylight. It was quite large—eight feet in length and five in width—and followed the slope of the roof. It offered a constantly shifting tableau. Only the ocean may be more fascinating to watch than clouds, and equally dangerous, for nothing is more useless and more deceptive and generally more stupefying than watching something that is ever changing and ever self-renewing. Yearning to describe, or understand, or even control it can cost you everything. What Virginie had first perceived as a long and sweetly amorous procession of clouds now contained an element of despair, unrequited love, and dreary solitude. She told herself that Richard Abercrombie's problem was that he had lacked loyal colleagues and admiring students; he never seemed to have had a true friend. He was not one of those men you could imagine being a child. He had been with hundreds of women, to whom he had devoted the most lyrical portions of his labors, yet without seeming ever to have known the true sweetness of togetherness. Sometimes Virginie no longer knew what to think. She was determined not to let this worry her. She had work to do.

At the Centre she regularly met with the top European meteorologists. From their conversations and from their replies to her questions, she learned that they viewed Richard Abercrombie as a colorful but ultimately pathetic figure from the distant past—the way an alchemist would seem to a modern chemist. As far as they were concerned, science was what was being done and thought now; what and who came before was immaterial. Nothing else existed, or no longer existed. Abercrombie's analogical science was, to them, an aberration.

They also tried and failed to understand why anyone would want to put clouds into rigid categories. Howard's system might still be of some utility to the enlightened amateur or the weekend painter, but nobody at Reading used it. Clouds had had their moment. The focus now was on describing atmospheric systems, the whole great totality of currents, depressions, and spiraling fronts. Gigantic and costly computers—working away in their silent, climate-controled, glass-partitioned rooms—were creating the maps of this new world.

Still, there was another way of looking at all this, and in the quiet of her little house Virginie struggled to articulate what it was. Abercrombie's analogical approach might well have evolved into a global and systematic conception of cloud behavior, because to him clouds were no longer separate and distinct entities but embodiments of the state of the atmosphere itself. Idiosyncrasy had taken his analogical system off course, that was true; he had, after all, built the altar of his private religion between the thighs of women. Virginie also believed that this was no more or less crazy a cult than any other. It had had few adherents in the world, fewer still in England. Of course Abercrombie could not have influenced contemporary meteorological research, given that his last work had not yet been made public. Yet Virginie couldn't help thinking that the simple fact he had discovered different ways of conceptualizing matter was significant in and of itself. She had arrived, from sheer determination, at a most satisfying paradox: A scientist had contributed decisively to making his own research seem aberrant by simultaneously showing how to transcend it.

———

Indifferent to fate, human or otherwise, science continued its forward progress. On March 5, 1950, in Aberdeen, Maryland, those forty-two computer banks designed by John Von Neumann, having been operated for thirty-three days and thirty-three nights by an international team of five experts, generated from a simplified model of the atmosphere three very specific forecasts that were valid for twenty-four hours. Von Neumann was the first to win the race of time between numeric calculations and natural forces. After that, things happened with ever greater speed, since the law of computers is the same as the law of the marketplace. The earth's atmosphere was divided up into a network of cubes, each reducible to a collection of points, and each point the product of a set of calculations. As far as science was concerned, this was the end of clouds, which were but a series of coordinates simulated in a space of greater than three dimensions.

A gigantic grid covered the earth's surface, the oceans, and the skies. Beginning in the 1960s satellites had been sent into the regions where terrestrial life cannot survive. A few of these satellites flew twenty thousand miles above the earth and moved at the same rotational speed, in geostationary orbit above the Equator—some in eternal light, therefore, and some in eternal darkness. Still other satellites brushed up against the atmosphere at a height of merely six hundred miles, following the shortest possible route along the axis between the two poles, which they crossed every twelve hours. At Reading and other places around the world, computers perform an unthinkable number of calculations every second. Hundreds of men and women have patiently constructed models based upon the parameters produced by the numeric method for forecasting, on earth as in the skies, because a very great deal needs to be factored in to make weather do what it does. On the ground, for example, were such things as snow-melt rates and heat reflection, plus all the variables, like geologic formation and topographical texture. There were the multiple interactions between the surface and the air, including those involving heat sensitivity and evaporation rates, as well as the phenomenon of friction. There were the atmospheric variations—humidity, temperature, and wind. And there were the physical processes going on within the atmosphere itself, such as diffusion, radiation, convection, and of course precipitation. All these had to be taken into account before anyone could deign to offer a forecast. Even after mastery of so many elements, researchers found they still had come up against an insurmountable wall, for despite the exponential increase in calculative speed it was virtually impossible to predict weather for a period greater than five days in larger areas, such as Europe. That was why the British Centre for Meteorological Forecasting in Reading had become the European Centre for Medium-Range Weather Forecasts.

Virginie was waiting for a storm. Every Monday when she arrived at the Centre she went straight into the forecasting room. Finally, on the first day of October, a powerful system was tracked to hit at the end of the week. It was moving from west of Ireland, churning its enormous mass. Virginie returned home the next evening, leaving early enough that the roads wouldn't be blocked.

According to calculations, when this storm hit the western coast of England it would be the largest in fifty years. On the morning of October 3, the experts couldn't believe what the numbers were telling them; the storm's dimensions surpassed anything they had ever seen. From London, where a special communications team had been set up, Virginie followed events. On the fourth, the Reading experts were completely perplexed, for the Centre had just put into service, after extensive preparation, a new generation of computer systems for predicting atmospheric conditions. The HV 1000 featured what is known as "distributive memory," which meant that it could perform a huge number of calculations through several memory operations, the goal being to produce a more sophisticated model. The Reading engineers had further improved upon the HV 1000's capacities by incorporating meteorological data from the previous decade, and then installing a separate search engine. Each time the HV 1000 issued a forecast, the second machine scoured its memory banks for previous conditions that most closely resembled the current ones and thus helped to amplify cartographic representation. Billions of calculations were stored in the distributive memory. Hence the computer could generate reliable predictions not simply for the next forty-eight or seventy-two hours but for the next eighty-four or even ninety-six hours. During a six-month trial period and one month of actual operation, this predictive trio—the HV 1000, the memory system, and the search engine—had provided incredibly precise and far-reaching forecasts.

During the first days of October this was the formidable system in place at Reading, though the older Fujitsu units were kept operational as well—just in case. And this was the system that starting on October 2 had been projecting precipitation rates and wind speeds so unbelievable that the database, which had been designed to invalidate results that moved beyond its range, refused to confirm them. In the control room, as they stood in front of the giant plasma screen, a screen large enough to permit a view of all the fronts approaching Western Europe, the meteorologists and technicians faced a dilemma so painful that they could barely look at one another. The Fujitsu machines were projecting wind gusts that were strong but still well within seasonal averages. Should they follow the HV 1000, a machine with greater capacities than any machine that had come before it, or fall back upon the older models and their more reasonable predictions? Such a decision could only be made following an intense discussion that also had to be brief—given that millions were waiting for their results—and hinged upon choosing between the tried-and-true and this new masterpiece of titanium and black carbon steel. They had invested five years of hard, underappreciated labor in it, costing the European community amounts too staggering to consider. The conclusion was in some ways a foregone one, given the fear of issuing a forecast based on unreliable information. They decided to use—without advertising the fact—the older machines. Therefore on the evening of October 3, the Centre at Reading issued a bulletin calling for a generally unstable weather system, with an advisory that wind speeds might reach level 2 on a scale of 6, with periods of heavy downpour and the possibility of hail. Nothing to get too alarmed about. This bulletin was posted on the Centre's official Web site and was automatically transmitted to registered users throughout Europe—institutions, transport companies, farms. Technicians began examining the HV 1000. In the early hours of the morning, they started receiving panicked calls from weather stations along the west coast of Ireland. A storm of massive dimensions, as large as Ireland itself, was preparing to cross it, moving east. It had turned slightly to the south and would bear down on England, the Belgian coast, and France. In Reading they clung to the hope that the winds would die down as rapidly as they had escalated. At around eight in the evening, the storm tore off the roofs of the housing for the Centre's administrators. By 9 P.M. they had to face the reality that they had under-forecasted the storm, though they were comforted in one aspect: The HV 1000 with distributive memory had not failed them.

Meanwhile, in London, as throughout the rest of England, the alert had been sounded. The streets were deserted, the houses shut up tight. After securing the shutters of her house, Virginie prepared to go out. That morning she had bought some bright yellow foul-weather gear. She left home at around four in the afternoon and, taking care to walk in the middle of the road, made her way toward the Heath. She knew perfectly well that this storm was deadly, that it would kill the careless and the shelterless. It would hurl cars into ditches, unleash lethal mud slides, and pull trees up by their roots. All this she knew with perfect clarity and still she couldn't keep from smiling at the thought that it had finally come—that even in the land of Richard Abercrombie there remained untamed powers. She stopped smiling when she reached the Heath; the wind was playing with her like a child's toy.

The important thing was to stay clear of the trees, so rather than take the winding wooded path, the one that locals and regular Heath-goers used, Virginie moved across the open fields. The tall grass that normally covered it had been pushed flat and was so slick that she could barely keep her footing. The sky was unrecognizable; grayish wisps whipped across it at incredible speed. Finally she reached the foot of Parliament Hill, which she ascended on her knees, deafened by the wind, blinded by the slashing torrents of rain. At the top she faced southeast, toward the city, whose outlines were blurred, as if submerged in molten lead. From the ventral pocket of her slicker Virginie took out a metal canister. She tried to open it slowly, ceremoniously, but the wind ripped open the top and in an instant scattered its contents. Virginie stared dumbly at the now-empty canister. In a burst of common sense, she realized that kneeling atop Parliament Hill she offered a perfect target for lightning, as well as for anything that happened to be flying through the air. She turned and began moving slowly back down the hill, braced against the wind.

It is sometime around five in the evening, and Virginie is in her house. She takes off her slicker and boots, draws a bath, removes her clothes, and settles into the warm water. She imagines that some of Akira Kumo's ashes may still be somewhere on the Heath, and they will nourish its trees. Some were probably shot straight up into the upper layers of the atmosphere and would not settle back down for quite some time. With a little luck, those ashes might ride upon one of the high-altitude currents that flow constantly above us at speeds greater than two hundred and fifty miles per hour, and which are the true authors of the weather down below. She imagines that some of these ashes might mingle with the remaining particles of Krakatoa's volcano, or even the vitrified traces, still radioactive, of a little girl vaporized on the banks of the Ota River. Virginie imagines all this while also thinking about her own port in this storm, this little white house where she will spend her life, which will be another story.